EMERGING VOICES

Volume 5

EMERGING VOICES

POETRY AND PROSE BY MARYLAND TEENS

VOLUME 5

Emerging Voices: Poetry and Prose by Maryland Teens
Copyright © 2020 Maryland Writers' Association. All rights reserved.
First Print Edition: September 2020

ISBN: 9798676253431

Maryland Writers' Association
Teen Writing Program
9466 Georgia Ave., #91
Silver Spring, MD 20910
www.marylandwriters.org

Editors: Henry Caballero, Roderick Deacey, Neal P. Gillen,
Christina L. Lyons, and Kari Ann Martindale
Cover and interior design and formatting by McGaughy Design

No portion of this book may be reproduced in any form or by any means, including electronic storage and retrieval systems, without the explicit prior written permission of the publisher. The characters and events in this book are fictitious. Any similarity to real persons, living or dead, is coincidental and not intended by the author.

CONTENTS

Preface i

When We Find Song *(Abby Kusmin)* 1

The Real Son *(Bianca Sauro)* 2

Carlota *(Lauren Arianna Raskin)* 12

Two Bros Chillin' on a Log in the Forest
    (Anna Grace O'Malley) 16

The Embalmer *(Nina Budinich)* 20

Eyes *(Aliya Peremel)* 28

The Elevens Curse *(Sydney Wu)* 30

Bennett Robs a Train *(Liberty Diaz)* 33

The Image *(Lily Madison)* 37

The Girl with the Butterfly Wings *(Abby Kusmin)* 41

Nameless Hero *(Zafar Mamat)* 42

Quarantine Thoughts *(Fatima Iqbal)* 52

Fate *(Sydney Wu)* 54

Strangers *(Nicole Hawks)* 56

Pandemic *(Siya Behl)* 61

Below *(Gillian Wesson)* 62

Midnight Bend *(Abby Kusmin)* 65

Get Out *(Fatima Iqbal)* 67

A Forest Corrupted *(Sydney Wu)* 73

Widow *(Anna Etienne)* 74

Shelved *(Fatimah Iqbal)* 75

Talisman *(Fiona McKee)* 81

A Bump in the Night *(Gillian Wesson)* 82

If Only I Had Listened *(Diana Karakunnel)* 90

Connecting Dots *(Margaret Cravens)* 94

My Name *(Lauren Arianna Raskin)* 97

A Helping Hand *(Ela Jalil)* 99

Acknowledgments 103

PREFACE

The following works represent a sampling of the young talent that the Maryland Writers' Association seeks to foster through its Teen Writing Clubs. Launched in 2009 with a single club outside Baltimore, the MWA now operates clubs around the state to nurture the creative writing talents of middle school and high school students. The clubs offer budding writers support, companionship, and feedback from peers, as well as guidance from adults in the writing field. The clubs also provide a setting for teens to celebrate achievements and discuss shared experiences and concerns.

Each volume of *Emerging Voices* includes poetry and prose in a variety of genres, including fantasy, realistic fiction, science fiction, and nonfiction. The teens often focus on a variety of topics, including love, grief, and loss. In this volume, several creative works reflect difficult topics that young people are striving to understand or to express in words. Racial and cultural divides continue to complicate social interactions in many communities. Gender identification is frequently a topic of discussion—in the media, in schools, and in families. In addition, many young people are struggling with anxiety and depression, witnessing the suffering of others, or coping with news about suicides in their communities. And in the year 2020, the coronavirus pandemic has closed schools and forced families, under government mandate, to quarantine at home, while cities have erupted with civil rights protests over police brutality targeted at blacks and other minorities. All of these issues are among the topics that are explored within this volume.

The stories were discussed and edited within club settings, and the editors for the book helped to guide the writers in refining their prose and poetry. We believe the stories reflect the teens' critical thinking and hopes for the future.

The teens in the MWA writing clubs don't all aspire to be professional writers, but they do all appreciate—and enjoy the rewards of—this creative craft.

The authors of the fifth volume of *Emerging Voices* include:

Siya Behl—Grade 11, Clarksburg High School
Nina Budinich—Grade 8, Lakelands Middle School
Margaret Cravens—Grade 9, Severn School
Liberty Diaz—Grade 10, Southern High School
Anna Etienne—Grade 11, Our Lady of Good Counsel High School
Fatimah Iqbal—Grade 11, Winston Churchill High School
Nicole Hawks—Grade 7, home school
Ela Jalil—Grade 10, Winston Churchill High School
Diana Karakunnel—Grade 11, Winston Churchill High School
Abby Kusmin—Grade 11, Montgomery Blair High School
Lily Madison—Grade 10, Southern High School
Zafar Mamat—Grade 8, Kingsview Middle School
Fiona McKee—Grade 10, home school
Anna Grace O'Malley—Grade 11, Montgomery Blair

High School
Aliya Peremel—Grade 9, Key School
Lauren Arianna Raskin—Grade 10, Poolesville High School
Bianca Sauro—Grade 12, Montgomery Blair High School
Gillian Wesson—Grade 11, Winston Churchill High School
Sydney Wu—Grade 9, Annapolis High School

Henry Caballero
Roderick Deacey
Neal P. Gillen
Christina L. Lyons
Kari Ann Martindale
Editors
August 2020

WHEN WE FIND SONG

By Abby Kusmin

I found it, a bird smaller than my palm
waiting for me in the tree,
singing through the smoke with its
faith that song will show us who to be.
I found it, a bird heavier than
all our grief, whose weight cannot stop it
from flying above all that we can see.
I found it, a bird with a heart fiercer than the sea,
its love great enough we might make it
through the fire to set ourselves free.

THE REAL SON

By Bianca Sauro

There were two rows of tired students between me and Nicholas Earle. The distance was miniscule, yet as he pushed his thick hair off his face and mumbled into the crappy auditorium microphone, he felt miles away.

Most of the students in the auditorium looked mildly bored. They knew the man speaking to them, or at least recognized the paintings that had been printed out and stuck haphazardly around the room to illustrate the cultural impact of the artist on stage. Still, the vast majority were rather apathetic towards the man. However, the teachers standing around the room were eagerly looking up at Mr. Earle.

It was a historic day for Alberta High School. By some stroke of luck, we had the privilege of becoming a stop on Nicholas Earle's speaking tour; some PR stunt or photo op, I'm sure. And I might be one of the luckiest of them all. Third row back out of fifty, three seats left of the middle aisle. Nicholas Earle had made fleeting eye contact with me twice now. Be still my beating heart.

He continued on about the power of reflection and art, speaking in a monotone without so much as a hint of a smile on his pale lips. My eyes wandered around the room, settling on a slideshow of Earle's most famous pieces.

Nicholas Earle's paintings used to be so beautiful to me. The slideshow flipped through his most famous pieces. Cherub-like, half-self-portraits of boys of all colors, creeds, builds, and physicalities. In each painting you could see a mirror of the artist's own features: Some had his striking blue eyes; others, his veiny hands with his long, gentle fingers; others, his hunched demeanor with broad shoulders and downcast eyes. But none had all of them; none looked exactly like the artist who had brought them to life.

His blue eyes would be paired with caramel skin, gentle hands on muscular arms, hunched back, and a sunshine smile. Creating chimeras, half himself, half some mystery woman, he painted to imagine what his son might look like, the one who escaped him all those years ago, taken by a woman he barely knew, a one-night stand gone wrong, a future that slipped through his hands.

It's all very tragic. Everyone agrees. The handsome, reclusive man from some town no one has heard of painting beautiful pictures of what his now teenaged son might look like, trying to capture some experience that he was robbed of all those years ago.

The story broke so many hearts that Earle was able to upgrade his studio, his apartment, his life. Now, he can pine over his long-lost son in the comfort of a penthouse estate, overlooking some big city, maybe with a skyline view, maybe a horizon. He can visit nowhere high schools and give lengthy speeches to exhausted students about those paintings that I used to think were so beautiful.

But none of them looked like me. I have his piercing blue eyes and his veiny hands, his long fingers, his broad shoulders, his downcast looks, and his bad habit of hunching that makes me seem sad even when I'm not. I tore my eyes away from the slideshow and forced myself to look at Nicholas Earle again. Small against the wooden podium, I imagined him melting under my gaze. His guesses were wrong, completely incorrect, absolutely useless pieces of shit that never helped anyone. But he remained a slave to the boys in the pieces, too busy adding freckles that I don't have to some preteen with stick-straight hair that I had always hoped for whenever I looked in a mirror, but never got.

He made eye contact with me again, and nothing changed in his eyes. No spark of recognition, not even surprise at this random kid who looked at him with such an unwavering glare. He had no idea who I was.

* * *

Mom looked at me with a concerned face before she spoke. "Marcus, I've something important to tell you." She paused to make sure she had my attention. "You're the son of Nicholas Earle."

Mom was always super direct. She didn't have time to waste, and often kindness was the casualty of practicality when it came to conversation.

Two months prior, some inconsequential Tuesday evening, right after dinner, she had given me the biggest news of my life, like it was no big deal.

"You're not serious."

I couldn't believe it. This was a man who became famous because he didn't know his son. And I, of all people, happened to be that kid? Unreal.

"You know I don't joke, Marcus."

She was washing the dishes so I couldn't see her face, but she sounded dead serious. And she did generally avoid kidding, but I wasn't going to believe her that easily.

"How do you know?" I asked, obviously skeptical.

"Marcus, I grew you. He's the only one who could be your father, unless you're the second Immaculate Conception…which I doubt."

Not much humor in that woman, but the sarcasm was always biting.

"Just look in the mirror if you don't believe me. You'll see it," she said.

She kept doing the dishes. I was stunned. Nicholas Earle was a household name, you have to understand. If I was his actual son…

"God, Mom, what do I do now? How long have you known? Why tell me now?"

She just shrugged in response, and that was the end of the conversation.

* * *

That day, I was just a face in a crowd of faces. The man on the stage didn't know. None of my schoolmates had any idea that I am Nicholas Earle's son. The Real Son, if you will. Medium: flesh, blood, bone, and one lucky sperm.

Months ago, I would have been elated to be sitting there in the auditorium, mere feet away from the painter who changed my life. Just the thought of hearing him drone on and on about texture and color and detail and heartbreak would have excited me out of my mind.

I used to love all of Earle's paintings. Like, all of them. He was actually a bit of a hero to me. I'm absolutely awful at art, but the paintings were enthralling, nonetheless. I printed them out in the school library and taped them in my locker, on my binder; put them up in my room. I think I was comforted by the fact that I wasn't the only one wondering about someone. Here I was imagining what my dad could look like and this big-name artist was wondering about his son. It was just a cool match. Turns out it was the match. At first it felt like a dream come true, but that quickly unraveled when I realized that Earle didn't give a shit about me. He had replaced me with canvases, oil paint, stippling brushes, and classical music.

"I believe that everyone is an artist and that everyone deserves a chance for their emotions to shine through music, watercolors, poetry, and the like. Art filled a hole in my life and made me a full person again. I hope it can do the same for you," Nicholas Earle said, concluding his speech, a small smile playing on his lips, the first one of the afternoon.

The teachers in the room erupted with applause, as did the students in the first three rows. They had saved the best spots for the art classes, and everyone around me was elated, eyes bright as new waves of inspiration filled their heads with big, unreachable dreams. They stood up, hooted and clapped, leaving me the only one sitting in a sea of ugly scarves and mismatched patterns. I clapped along unenthusiastically, staring at the floor. He said that art filled a hole in his life. A hole that was me. A hole that was my mother. A hole he could have actually filled if he had tried. But he didn't. He just filled the hole with paint and let it dry.

The auditorium began clearing out. The teachers rounded up their classes, trying to maintain organization and garner some semblance of respect at the end of the school day. I stayed sitting, surrounded by my art classmates and reeling.

"You good, Marcus?" To my left, my friend Vincent looked down at me with concern.

"Yeah, I'm good. Just weird seeing Earle in person. Lots of emotions," I replied, forcing an eyeless smile.

"Totally get it, dude. He's, like, the artist of our generation, and he was maybe three steps away. Freakin' insane." Vincent ran a hand through his hair and chuckled to himself. He was the one who originally introduced me to Earle just before his popularity skyrocketed. Everyone in the class liked Earle, but Vincent loved the man. When Mom told me that Nicholas Earle was my father, the only person I wanted to tell was Vincent. But I knew I couldn't. It would be too complicated.

I pulled myself out of the chair and filed out of my row. I had a headache. Mr. Wilson, our art teacher, approached the clump of students that made up his class. Many were wiping away tears, some were jumping around with a fire in their eyes, a few yawned, but the twenty-five of us were clearly the least apathetic of the student body.

"How are you guys holding up?" Mr. Wilson asked with a smile. He looked at Vincent, who grinned in response.

"That was amazing, Mr. Wilson, really. It's a good day for Alberta High," Vincent laughed.

The class was almost alone in the auditorium. The school day was about half an hour away from ending, and we were all prepared to return to the art room, grabbing coats and rubbing tired eyes, reconvening around our teacher. Vincent started to lead the way out of the room until Mr. Wilson grabbed his shoulder.

"I have a surprise for you guys," he said with a smile. "I convinced Mr. Earle's manager to schedule him for a private meet-and-greet after his speech. He's going to come back out here in a few minutes. I hope you don't mind ending the school day a little early."

My heart plummeted. I imagined it hitting my stomach and dissolving into a bubbling acidic mess.

My classmates cheered and jumped around me. Vincent looked like he was going to explode. Tears leaked out of his wide eyes, and he put an arm around my shoulder, squeezing me tightly.

"Holy shit, holy shit, holy shit," he whispered, half to me and half to himself. "Damn, I can't make a fool of myself. I need a script, a list of questions; I need to prepare."

A chorus of "thank-yous" rang out from the class as we walked back to the front row of chairs and took our seats. My leg bounced in anticipation that I assumed my classmates interpreted as excitement. I guess it kind of was. It was everything. They were meeting an idol. I was meeting a parent. Half of my genetics. I was meeting my blue eyes and gentle hands and slumped shoulders.

Nicholas Earle walked through the double doors at the front of the room, and the class cheered. Everyone was on their feet as he came over to us. Even I stood. My heart sloshed around in my stomach. I felt sick. Nicholas Earle was not an intimidating figure. His face was angular and his features were defined. If he held himself up taller, radiated confidence instead of caution, he would have been handsome. But he walked slowly and talked in a monotone and made himself small. The smile on his thin lips as he greeted my classmates made it evident that he was prideful. He knew that he was good, looked up to.

He went down the row, shaking hands. When he got to me, I thought that I might throw up. His hands grasped mine. They were almost the same. My skin was darker and smoother, his pale and tough. His eyes met mine and they were the same. Piercing, crystal blue.

"Hello, young man, what's your name?" he asked.

"Marcus Stewart," I heard myself respond. I could feel my hand shaking in his.

"Are you an artist, Marcus?"

"No, sir. I just like looking." I could hear my heart thundering in my ears.

"Nothing wrong with that," he chuckled. And then he

moved on.

The rest of the meet-and-greet moved with merciful swiftness. Vincent cried and stumbled over questions. Earle gave him a hug and answered each one in detail. Some of the class members took out prints of his work, and he signed each one with a personal note to the student. I sat in silence, watching and doing my best to look enthused.

When the final bell rang, he shook each of our hands one more time. I only glanced at him this time, giving his hand a quick squeeze before pulling away. Vincent cried again, and Earle gave him another hug.

"Keep painting, Vincent," I heard him say. "There's no hole that can't be filled with art."

The class began to file out as Nicholas Earle headed back through the double doors from which he came. I walked with Vincent, taking deep calming breaths. I heard the double doors open as Earle slipped out of my life. Damn.

I turned around and sprinted towards the door as it closed behind Earle.

"Marcus!" Mr. Wilson shouted as I blew past him. I threw open the door and almost slammed into the painter.

"What's the rush? Marcus, isn't it? Good name, I ..." he sputtered.

"I'm your son. Your actual son." I blurted out. "I'm the son of Mary Stewart—average height, curly hair, tan, really direct—a little mean actually. She honestly probably left as soon as she knew she was pregnant with me. She has a hard time trusting."

"Marcus, Marcus," he said, trying to stop me. "I'm sorry, kid, but do you know how many people claim to be my son? I want to believe you, but I can't. I'm truly sorry. I hope you find you father; I do. But it's not me, kid, it's not me."

He grasped my hand and pulled me in for a hug. I was dumbfounded. Speechless.

"Take care of yourself, Marcus. I always liked that name," he said, taking a last look into my eyes—his eyes. Then he walked away, leaving me standing in the dimly lit hallway, confused and betrayed.

* * *

The printer whirred as it struggled to capture the details and colors of the painting. It did a decent job; I was happy with it. I opened up the frame and slipped the paper inside, closing the clasps.

Mom was in the kitchen making lunch.

I took the framed piece of paper and hung it on a nail in the middle of the kitchen wall. Mom turned around and took a look at it.

"That is the ugliest painting I have ever seen," she said, turning back around.

"My thoughts exactly," I responded with a smile.

* * *

Two years ago, I had met Nicholas Earle at the peak of his career. It was all downhill from there for the poor guy. The tragedy started wearing off. His paintings were good, but he could only make so many guesses, have so many sons, before the gag became stale.

Now, he's old news. A one-night stand for the art community. Pushed out a few good pieces, got a few years of fame, and sputtered out. I look at the painting I just put up.

It's his self-proclaimed last painting, ever. Didn't get

much attention from critics. But I like it. It depicts a tall, tan boy with curly hair, gentle hands, blue eyes, and slumped shoulders standing in a hallway. The yellow light around him makes him look even more forlorn than the expression of disbelief on his face. He's wearing a dark blue hoodie with a high school crest on the breast.

Nicholas Earle signed this piece in the bottom left corner, the title of the piece accompanying his name: "The Real Son."

CARLOTA

By Lauren Arianna Raskin

Her classmates always seemed to find it immensely difficult to pronounce her name. Their lips would stumble drunkenly about the soft vowels, and their teeth would clank together as they spat out the rigid consonants. They would say her name as if the very word left a sour taste in the back of their mouths. Carlota? Always with their tone stretching toward the sky in disbelief, always as a question.

When she first came to the States, a stubborn tan from the Mexican sun having yet to fade, she would try to correct them. Just as her mama would tell her, she would say that the mouth should cradle the word as if it were a newborn baby. That it should sit loosely on the tongue like a piece of hard candy. They never cared, but she always did. She knew the meaning of her name like the creases of her palm, like she knew the smell of her papa after he returned home from the picking fields, a subtle earthy aroma, so distinct it was as if he were made of all the elements of nature themselves. She loved her name.

Until one day she didn't.

One day, it became yet another thing that set her apart from everyone else, like the dark hair that shot out of her arms, weeds that grew out of the soil that was her skin. Her skin that was at least three shades darker than that of everyone else in school, contrasting severely among the sea of ivory-colored legs and arms and faces. These are the differences that painted a shiny target across her back and paved a trail of racist comments as she walked through the halls of school.

Your people aren't wanted.

She would scream back at them, her body shuddering under the weight of her fury, until her mouth ran dry and her voice went hoarse. She would scream and scream and scream until the world around her became a heap of dust beneath her feet, until the raging sea that churned in the pit of her stomach lapsed into calm, pulsing waves. But they would never hear her. Because here, inside her mind, Carlota would simply squeeze her eyes shut and push their words to the darkest corner, praying that she could drown out the demons that lunged for her throat. Oh, how she missed Mexico. She longed for the days of working in her family's *panaderia* alongside her mama, the smell of freshly baked tortillas tickling the underside of her nose. Or how in the midst of the humid summer, she and her little sister would scale the orchid trees that littered her town, climbing so high it felt as if their fingertips could brush against the clouds that hung low in the sky. She felt unstoppable then. But that was before, and she was living in after. I will come back one day, she promised herself, back to the days of freedom.

For now, Carlota would remain a prisoner, her hands and feet not bound by iron shackles, but by the demons that whispered in her ears. Why don't you go back to the fields where you belong? Stupid Mexican.

Carlota was not stupid. No, not stupid at all. She prided herself on her mind, in fact. It was her papa who drilled into her the importance of education; he was often teased that he had shoved a book in Carlota's hand the second she burst out of her mama's belly, before the nurse could even confirm the presence of ten fingers and ten toes.

"Oh, *Dios mío*! What a smart girl you are!" he once exclaimed when Carlota returned home from school in Mexico, a paper clutched in her hand with the letter A scrawled on top. Carlota still remembered how he swaddled her body in an embrace, his arms clasped tightly together over the hunch of her shoulders and the crook of his neck perched upon her head, like a sparrow in a nest. They fit together like puzzle pieces, just as a papa and his daughter should.

"You make me very proud, *mija*. You are smart, you will accomplish great things in life. Get a good job. Don't have hands like mine." And he showed Carlota his hands. Though he was just a few months shy of his thirtieth birthday, his hands were those of a much older man, the broad back sides mottled with patches of sun-bleached skin. Papa had labored in the fields for as long as Carlota could remember and as long as he could remember too. He would rise when night began to bleed into day and would begin working before the sun even had time to wipe the sleep out of his eyes. Carlota still found beauty in his hands. They told a story of suffering, the turmoil between the force of man and the unwavering might of nature. But his calluses and discolored flesh also traced a map, one of dedication and hope. Papa was intelligent, and so was Carlota. Which is why it pained her when she was called anything less, why her soul split into a million pieces when "stupid Mexican" was hollered at her from across the hall. But she would swat away their words like the tail of a horse flicking away flies and continue walking on.

She walked like a soldier, with purpose, never breaking speed, all while her hands clamped so tightly around the frayed strap of her satchel that her knuckles shone white. Not with fear would they shine—not anymore—but with determination. She had the strength of her family behind her, generations of sweat, blood, and sacrifice that led her to where she was that day. She would learn to love America as she loved Mexico, and she would carry the two countries in her heart wherever she went.

I am Mexican. I am American. I am Carlota.

TWO BROS CHILLIN' ON A LOG IN THE FOREST

By Anna Grace O'Malley

Long, long ago, in a world very different from the one we know today, two bros sat five feet apart on a log in the forest. They waited for the flowers to bloom, the flowers that grew on vines above them but had never seen the light of day. For as long as the flowers had lived, the world had been shrouded in an eternal darkness, unyielding to all but those few who could summon light. The flowers had lived centuries longer than these two bros, who had never known light either. All they had known was to listen, to smell, to touch, and to taste. They could not differentiate between colors. If explained to them by an ancient being, they would not even be able to comprehend what it must be like to see.

One of the bros heard a rustle to his left, where the other bro sat. He reached across the five feet of space and grabbed the other bro's hand. He gave his hand a reassuring, platonic squeeze.

"She said to wait, but how will we know when the flowers have bloomed?" asked the first bro. "I cannot reach them or smell them through all the other aromas in this forest. Can you sense them, Ali?"

"They are faint, but yes," answered Ali, who had another sense little known to any but the two bros. "When they open, my awareness of them will bloom just as they do. Right now it is shriveled, a collection of potential waiting to be released."

"What are we to do once they have bloomed? All she told me was to wait with you. But what use is my being here when your sense is all that we need?"

"You are here to keep me company, Shea. I would be afraid by myself in these woods, startled by every rustle of leaves or twig snapped under a small creature's heel.

"But Ali, if my purpose is to comfort you, why do we sit so far apart?"

There was a pause as Ali considered this.

"I don't know," he finally responded.

Then he bridged the gap between them, shrinking the five feet to nothing. Their hands had lost each other somewhere in the midst of their conversation, but they found each other again. A small comfort in the dark forest filled with the unknown, but any comfort is a significant one in times of doubt.

"Now we wait," said Ali.

As the seconds, minutes, hours passed by, Ali noticed how his senses were altered by Shea's presence beside him. He felt Shea's hand in his, his body beside him, his scent of the sweet fruits he spent his time gathering. He heard the rhythmic shifting of Shea's feet brushing the leaves below, an occasional word or two of comfort spoken by the other bro. But most notably, with Ali's extra sense, he couldn't help focusing on Shea rather than the flowers above. With his mind, he could trace the outline of his cheek, turned toward a gentle gust of wind. He was aware of the way Shea's lips tilted up at the corners when he spoke to Ali. He knew that his own presence was also a comfort to Shea.

But Ali worried of the mission. How could he commit his senses to the blooming flowers above rather than the bro beside him?

Ali wondered if he should move away, reinstate the former five feet between them.

"Ali?" asked Shea. "Are you okay?"

"I think so," Ali said. "But how did you know something was wrong?"

"I felt you tense up beside me. And I just had a feeling. But I don't know how to describe it to you. It was a shape, something solid and cold, something unsure of itself. And somehow I knew it pertained to you."

Ali thought about this for a minute. This sounded like his own extra sense, but how could Shea perceive what only Ali knew? Ali focused his thoughts on the woods for a moment. His awareness blossomed until he could feel the coiling bark of the trees, their complex layers within; feel the fur of the creatures sleeping in the hollows; crumble fallen leaves with a tendril of thought. This was more than Ali had ever been able to do. He was used to observing, not altering.

Ali turned to Shea and took his other hand. "Can you feel that?" he asked.

"Yes," said Shea in wonder. "I can feel everything."

Ali could feel the world around him as he normally observed it, but alongside Shea, he could feel Shea's perception of the forest, the ability passed to him by their interwoven hands. Shea's perception alongside his own made Ali feel as if all the boundaries he had known had faded to nothing. He felt limitless, powerful, infinite. Was this how the ancient ones felt when the world was illuminated and they could see?

"I think I can make the flowers bloom," said Ali.

"We can make the flowers bloom," corrected Shea.

Ali felt a burst of power as Shea squeezed his hands. He was boundless; he could do anything. He reached his thoughts all the way up to the vines above, sending power flowing through them. His awareness melded with Shea's and kept adding more and more power to the vines. Then they directed it all into the flower buds, and all at once, their awareness exploded with pink.

The flowers blossomed with light, and Ali and Shea could see. Before, they had only a faint awareness of shapes, but this was true vision. Together, they had re-created the world of old.

THE EMBALMER
By Nina Budinich

Cecil was different. There was no denying it.

Even when they were a small child, found at the brink of the woods all on their own, their parents could feel something off about them. Something about the way that they watched people with those sharp silver eyes, constantly judging, constantly questioning their genuineness. Something about the way that they'd sit in the background of a conversation for an hour or so, and you just couldn't ignore that they were there.

Oh, and there was another thing.

Their skin was pale as death.

This put everyone on edge. Death was a very sacred, very tentative topic. Everyone feared that death would come and sweep someone they loved off of their feet and into the Great Unknown. To even speak about death could make an entire room go silent as if the person would simply die right there on the spot.

Given that Cecil's skin was almost as pale as that of a fresh corpse, no one was particularly comfortable around them. People avoided them.

And to be completely and absolutely honest, Cecil didn't mind at all.

They were hardly eleven years old when people started picking on them for the gloves and face mask. The face mask was easily explained. The gloves, not so much. The other children at school would relentlessly annoy them, and Cecil was happy when their learning days were finally over and they could be on their own.

As Cecil pushed open the door to their work space, they inhaled the scent of embalming herbs and set down their leathery black case, a gift from their adoptive mother. Sunlight filtered in through the many small windows and illuminated the sharp, shiny tools that soon would be put to good use. Cecil flipped the sign on the door to "Open" and waited. Though the days weren't always bountiful, they still enjoyed the quiet of the shop, how no one was there to talk to them and be the fakest person that they could possibly be.

Face-to-face interaction was difficult. Fake. You take a person's opinion and bounce it off of you. Cecil decided to dwell on this as they waited.

It was only about ten minutes before a person was at the door. "Come in," Cecil called quietly.

The mahogany door opened, revealing a woman with red eyes and stained cheeks. There was an intricately embroidered handkerchief in her shaky dark hands, knuckles white from clutching it so hard. Cecil immediately knew that this woman was a mother.

"I've heard that you…deliver the dead," the mother whispered, voice trailing off at the end as if she herself couldn't believe the rumors that spread across the village like wildfire.

Cecil nodded while adjusting their face mask. "I do. I don't suppose that's the reason you've come?"

The mother clutched her embroidered handkerchief closer to her chest and nodded. "I've also heard that you can…bring them…"

"Back?" Cecil finished, already standing up. "You're correct. Lead me to your home, and I'll see what I can do."

The journey across the village certainly wasn't long.

Or at least, it shouldn't have been. By the time they were halfway there, Cecil realized that they were going to the servants' quarters, the quarters for the royal maidens. They'd never dealt with a royal servant before. *The reward should be quite fruitful*, Cecil thought with an almost-smile on their face as they dashed through the halls.

Once they came upon the entry to the servants' quarters, the mother was out of breath. Cecil, perfectly adapted to this kind of exercise, turned to the mother expectantly and raised a thin black eyebrow. "Which room is he in?"

"Four," the mother gasped, leaning against a pillar. "Please. Don't let my son go. You can't let him stay dead."

"Don't worry, *m'laire*," Cecil reassured, considering patting her arm but deciding against it. "I won't."

They swept through the warm hall, reading the small carvings of numbers as they went. One, two, three, four. Other servants bustled through the hall, looked at them, looked away, looked backed again. This only made Cecil more determined to get the job over with. Stopping in front of the door to room four, Cecil didn't bother to knock as they went inside. Four twin beds…set up across from each other in a double-plus pattern. Light shone through the white curtains, giving the room a balanced feeling of comfort and homeliness. The servants knew how to make a home.

A few people were gathered at one of the bedsides, murmuring to themselves. Awkwardly, Cecil cleared their throat. The servants glared at the embalmer before leaving. As soon as the room was empty they felt lighter.

There was a boy on the bed, his sharp face empty of expression and his eyes closed. It almost looked like he was asleep. Cecil had seen enough of these things to know that he wasn't. A shame, really. He looked like such a healthy boy. When their eyes caught sight of the black and white pendant around his neck, they forced their eyes away. They put a gloved hand on his dark forehead and closed their eyes. Sickness. That was easily cured, no mess and no fuss. Many people die of sickness nowadays.

Brushing a short lock of ebony wavy-curly hair out of their face, recapturing it into its silver clip, the embalmer set to work.

First they ensured that the grey gloves on their hands were secure, and then they opened their case. It was a simple case on the outside, but within, it was endless, filled with many useful things: bandages, wraps, glues, poisons, matches…syringes of all kinds.

Pulling out a clean, thin syringe, Cecil rolled up their sleeve. This part used to really bother Cecil, but not anymore. In fact, it was rather comforting to feel a pinch every now and then, helping to ensure that they were still awake.

Without any further ado, the embalmer removed a bit of blood.

The sting only lasted for a few seconds as they expertly took exactly one milliliter of blood into the syringe. Rolling up the dark green of the boy's sleeve, Cecil injected the syringe and pushed down the plunger.

Anyone outside looking in would think that this was absolutely disgusting and inhumane. What kind of person injected their own blood into someone else, especially after they were dead? Cecil, apparently.

After the last few drops of crimson substance disappeared beneath the boy's skin, Cecil took out the syringe, cleaned it off, put it back into the case, and clasped their hands on their lap and waited. This was a short process, and it was always nice to be there when they woke up. Besides, it was quite the show.

The light started slow, but it blossomed along his veins and arteries very nicely from the spot of injection. The light burned off any illness that remained in his cold body, leaving only a warm lavender glow coursing through his bloodstream. The light made it to his brain, and it started up again. It went through his insides, reigniting the spark that illness had snuffed out. Finally, the light gathered around his heart, and it started pumping again.

The boy woke up as the light burst off of him. Job finished.

The boy looked around, very confused. His cocoa eyes widened as he scanned the room, eyes stopping on Cecil. They stared at each other for a few seconds before the boy croaked, "Water?"

The embalmer didn't even hesitate to get up and get him a glass of water. Once the boy had gulped the water down, he whispered, "Mother?"

"She's outside," Cecil nodded, taking his hand in theirs, helping him up, and leading him out. The boy stared at his hands, amazed. People were like that when they came back—amazed, frightened, stunned, sometimes angry. Mostly, they were disoriented.

As soon as they set foot outside, the boy jolted to a stop. Cecil bumped into him, almost falling over. Then they looked up.

King Angevin. He was right there, standing outside of the room. He stared down at Cecil with warm brown eyes, the light that their piercing silver eyes broke through. He was in full royal attire, a bit overwhelming for someone as small as Cecil. The mother stood behind him, eyes wide and glistening with fresh tears as she sputtered, "T-Tedros?"

"Mother," the boy, Tedros, breathed as a smile split his features. He ran, almost stumbling, towards her, arms wide. "Mother!"

As the two embraced, Cecil folded their arms. Another job flawlessly completed. King Angevin watched the exchange, a small smile floating under his moustache. "You certainly know how to bring joy upon a family, don't you?"

Cecil fidgeted with their gloves, feeling the stares of other servants burning through their skull. They hated being the pinpoint of attention, especially after, y'know, bringing someone back from the Unknown.

The king noticed the discomfort and patted their back, making them jump. With a chuckle, the king started walking away and gestured for them to follow. The two of them left the servants' quarters and slowly made their way through the palace. Cecil gripped their case tightly as they admired the scenery. Stopping on a large bridge with a splendid view of the village, the king asked, "What do you call that strange power?"

"Power?" Cecil parroted, voice no more than a whisper. It was a blessing and a curse how quietly they spoke. Peaceful and calm. Docile and fragile. "You mean… necromancy?"

King Angevin nodded once. "Yes. Necromancy. The act of defying death itself." A pause as he looked out into the horizon. The rising sun outlined his thick auburn moustache and his silver crown. "Defying death. Bringing someone back from the Unknown. It's unheard of. Unnatural." He turned to Cecil. "Tell me. How far does this ability go?"

They flicked the clasps of their case. "If I can fix the body, then I can recover the Soul."

The king hummed in understanding, resting his hands on the railing. Cecil did the same, though they weren't nearly as tall as him. "When Sarah's child, Tedros, passed from Scorching Heart Disease, the first thing that her brother told her to do was 'Go to the embalmer.' As if they'd fix everything." A small smile. "You did, didn't you?"

Cecil's mouth tightened under their mask. "Almost."

He raised his eyebrows. "Almost?"

"He won't live as long as he normally would; if he hadn't died from SHD," the embalmer said, trying to find their home in the fray of buildings below. "Of course, I could keep coming back and bringing him back to life."

"So you can bring people back multiple times?" King Angevin asked, voice suddenly filled with hope. It was almost childish hope, the kind of hope that you'd see in a kid who was just told that they could have any kind of candy in the store. It was almost like that, but much more…mature. Fatherly.

"Yes," Cecil said, rubbing their arms now as if to feel the spots where the needle punctured their skin. "If I can find their Soul."

The king turned to them abruptly. His cocoa-colored eyes glittered with hope. "If I may interest you, I have an offer."

The offer was so sudden that Cecil almost dropped their case. "An—an offer?"

King Angevin nodded aggressively, crown almost falling off of his head. "My daughter, Princess Pandora. If you can serve as her life support, then we will be eternally indebted to you."

Cecil's head was spinning now. *Princess Pandora? The one that no one's ever seen in public?* "Why…why would you want me to support your daughter?" they asked.

"We will explain in full later," the king said with a tone suggesting he couldn't believe his luck. Cecil certainly couldn't believe theirs. "If you take my offer, you shall be well cared for the rest of your days. No harm shall ever come to you again. You will be launched into society and never feel discomfort again. Do you accept this offer?"

It was a fairly easy decision. As long as Cecil was there to bring his daughter back to life whenever she needed it, they'd be forever comforted. Cecil took the king's hand into their gloves, giving it a firm shake. "Yes."

The king told them to come back to the palace the next day and to bring all of their things with them. As they walked away, Cecil finally felt some sort of freedom. They were finally going to be left alone! They could finally live in comfort without people staring at them as they brought people back, day in and day out.

After all, it was the princess.

They stopped in their tracks, suddenly feeling even lighter than before. Pandora Angevin. They were going to be right next to the princess at all times, ready to resurrect her. That was, unless their power was suddenly…faulty.

Princess Pandora Angevin. The one Soul that they were destined to reap.

EYES

By Aliya Peremel

I thought your eyes were dark
black and mysterious
reflecting the universe
but I was wrong
they are as amber as the sunset
setting the world on fire
burning even after the dusky evening glow turns the spark to ashes

I thought your eyes were blue
as deep as the ocean
reflecting the sky
but I was wrong
they are streaked with yellow
lightning striking the soft earth
reminding everyone there is a strength within your calm

I thought your eyes were hazel
as mixed and changing as your thoughts
reflecting the summer mirage
but I was wrong
they are as green as spring grass
olives extending from the tree
reminding you to find growth even in the most barren of places

I thought your eyes were chestnut
warm and inviting
showing the kind side of you that nobody cares to see
but I was wrong
they are a dusty gold
shining in the sunlight
misty and overflowing
ever changing
signifying the fluidity of your emotions
showing there is so much more to you than meets the eye

I thought your eyes were striking
a vivid cerulean
but I was wrong
they are a faded slate
reflecting your sadness back at the world
dull and grey
reminding everyone of who you were and will never be again

THE ELEVENS CURSE
By Sydney Wu

Mara stood staring at the clock, ticking, ticking, ticking. The hand passed the big ten, to the eleven, and stayed there. She looked away. The ticking continued, luring her back.

She resisted the urge to look and turned away.

Eleven, a cursed number in her heart. A tender ache still throbbing. It used to be her lucky number, but now it was only a burden. It resurfaced, hauntings of memory that she once desperately tried to bury. Eleven.

Eleven pairs of shining eyes, eleven big smiles, eleven with not a care in the world. She saw her face among them. She shook her head, as if to get the thoughts out. The ache throbbed harder. She looked back at the clock, hearing it tick, but the hand stayed, paralyzed on the number.

She drowned in the ticking. The clock's endless melodies seeping into her brain. Angered shouting and yelling echoed from the past to the present. A fight to end all fights. Pillows flying, a river of tears, streaming, streaming. Streaming from her eyes even now. Eleven streams. Eleven seas parting. Eleven down to one.

She looked back around her empty apartment. The bare walls, stripped of paint, the creaky unstable floorboards, the messy main room, the unmade bed, and the clock. Once the walls were plastered with photos and memories, but she buried those memories and burned those photos. Eleven faces burning in her mind's eye.

The ache grew even more, building up the pain in her

heart. The tears wouldn't stop. Eleven separated by fate's cruel hands and placed so far away, there was no hope of return. She banged her fists against the wall and collapsed to her knees. The clock swung on its nail and crashed to the ground. The glass shattered across the floor, and the rest of the clock landed face up.

She sat in the middle of broken glass and stared at the clock in front of her, ticking, ticking, ticking. Her body was covered in bleeding cuts, the crimson streaks tattooed onto her skin. Tears landed onto the scarred face of the clock, mixing with the blood and making it spread. She still stared, the ticking, ticking, ticking at the still unmoving eleven.

She diverted her gaze for just a second and stared at the blood-stained glass fragments surrounding her. She slowly reached for one and picked it up. She ran her finger over the sharp edge, turning her eyes back to the clock.

Ticking, ticking, ticking. The eleven filled her eyes and that's all she could see. She closed them, but the number was still burned onto her eyelids. She ran her finger over the edge of the shard again. The ache in her heart beating and beating, throbbing and throbbing.

She moved her arm in a slow arc until the glass was placed against her wrist. Her ears filled with ticking, ticking, ticking. And she sliced.

* * *

Her eyes opened with bright light shining through fuzzy vision. A soft hospital bed was sturdy beneath her. Soft noises brushed her ears, whispers from far away. Ten pairs of dimmed eyes hovered above her face. They pierced through the haze, and her eyes focused.

She was in a hospital room, looking up, ten faces contrasting the white ceiling. She stared into the once-bright eyes from resurfaced memories, and smiles turned to worried frowns.

"Hey, we came to visit." The voice brought her back. She closed her eyes again as the tears returned and streamed down her face.

She reached up as if to touch their faces, but her arm was covered in bandages. Across her whole body there were bandages, stitches, and wounds. She opened her eyes, then remembered.

The tears just came down harder. Surrounded by ten pairs of shining eyes, ten worn out smiles.

Now one was eleven once more.

BENNETT ROBS A TRAIN
By Liberty Diaz

The stars were already out over the desert when Bennett and I lit the dry kindling with a simple fire-starting charm from my pocket. I reached into my bag and pulled out two apples, tossing one to him. He nodded gratefully and took a bite.

"Have I ever told you about Mull's Bridge?" he asked, wiping some juice from his chin. I thought about it and shook my head. "You've probably heard it, just not from me. Every paper covered it, from all the way out here to over in Adams."

"That was you?" I was shocked. To be fair, I should've put two and two together earlier. It's exactly the kind of reckless and stupid thing he'd do with his power.

He laughed. "What, you didn't think I could make off with that much money? Come on, Colin. I don't just busy myself with commercial coaches. Sometimes, I have a bit more flair," he said, waving his hands dramatically.

"I'm sure there are things the paper left out," I said, leaning back on a rock, ready to hear another one of Bennett's wild adventures. He finished his apple and pitched the core down the hill.

"I was robbing a train—alone, mind you—down south, where they have all those mountains and mesas and rock spires. It was the Lewis Whitehall Express." He paused for a moment to allow me to be impressed. "It was taking those rich folk through empty country to some cushy resort on the lake. Couldn't have been more perfect. My contact didn't send me a ticket—should have been a red flag from the start. Problem was, I didn't have the cash to pay for one."

"What? Did you lie or threaten your way into one?"

"No interruptions, please." He shot me an exaggerated glare, then resumed. "Luckily, the station clerk was some gullible kid. I finally got a chance to test my story about my dying forbidden lover and how I needed to see her immediately. The poor romantic fool gave me a ticket and, after I pleaded with him, he swore that he wouldn't tell my fictional darling's fictional family that I'd come that way. I was finally on the train. Once we were well out of town, I held up the two passenger cars, collecting what I came for, before the conductor could notice. Not much in the way of resistance or security. That's certainly changed since then," he laughed mischievously. "So, I jumped off the train onto a plateau. Before I could inspect the loot, I saw something coming towards me." He stopped to toss another twig onto the fire. "Blue-coated lawmen. A whole lot of them, too. Obviously, my contact had set me up. I panicked and started running along the tracks and found myself on Mull's Bridge. There were even more lawmen coming from the other side. I was trapped."

I remembered this next part from the newspaper, but I was excited to hear it directly from Bennett. I took a drink from my canteen. "Go on," I said, urging him to continue his story.

"I was standing on this bridge with the law closing in on me, holding one of the biggest hauls of my entire life.

There was no way to go off either side of the bridge, I'd be shot, certainly, but I had a great idea.

"A stupid idea," I said.

"An amazing idea," he said as he rolled his eyes. "I waited for the law to come right up to me, because, if I ended up dead, I wanted to do it as memorably as possible. The sheriff rode up on a big white horse and started his 'surrender or we'll shoot' spiel. Everyone had rifles aimed steady. 'Hello, sir,' I shouted, 'if you could just lower your weapons, then maybe we could negotiate, like the civil men we are.' That old fool just spat his tobacco juice, squinted, and drew his revolver. 'Last chance, scum.'"

"Did he really say that?" I couldn't help cutting in at that point in his story.

Bennett cocked his head. "Were you there?"

I laughed and waved for him to continue.

"I took my hands off my guns, put them behind my head and started backing up towards the edge of the bridge." Bennett closed his eyes, relishing the memory.

"Is this where you dropped your little dime novel one-liner?"

"It was the best I could think of at the moment. Put yourself in my situation," he said, obviously offended.

I scoffed. "Stop defending your lack of humor and keep going."

"I was standing at the edge of the bridge, at least thirty people with guns pointed at me. I flung my hat into the air with as much flair as I could muster and yelled, 'Say a prayer for me, boys!'"

"And?"

"And then I leaped down into Mull's Gorge with a bag

of billfolds and diamond wedding rings."

I pictured the canyon, a massive gash between two mesas. Seven stories deep, and Bennett's first instinct was to jump down into it. Most of the time, I wasn't sure if he was a reckless genius or just a lucky idiot. "How'd you survive the fall?" I asked.

He smiled confidently at the memory. "About halfway down I shifted, you know, into smoke. Never done it so fast since. Probably because I was a few seconds away from dying at the bottom of a canyon. Either way, when I was safe at the bottom, I became myself again. I grabbed the bag of goodies and got as far away as possible. I guess they thought I was dead."

Bennett shrugged, but there was a touch of playful pride in his eyes. "Lost that hat. It was a nice one, too."

I shook my head. "Sometimes I wonder if being around you is good for my own self-preservation."

"Probably not. But I do make good company."

"I'd rather hear your stories than be a part of them, that's certain."

He sighed, staring up at the stars. "I know you aren't interested in working with me. You know, robbing, but if you ever wanted to…" He trailed off. "I could use a partner that won't stab me in the back."

Good luck, Bennett.

THE IMAGE

By Lily Madison

What do you do when there is no escape? When, even in your dreams, you can see the end. When all day there is an Image sitting in the back of your mind, whether you're eating breakfast or making conversation. That Image breaks through the walls of focus, and the harder you try to block it out, the clearer it becomes. It is the one thought in your consciousness, always there, always ready to reveal some new horror to you when you are most unprepared. And even when you are prepared, when you have been thinking of how to stop it for so long you cannot remember anything else, it will still shock you with its brutality.

But where does the Image come from? Well, no one really knows. For some, it is something present from childhood, something put into your unformed mind by a sadistic elder. For others, it will just appear one day and never leave. For me…for me, it was strange. Mine was first an idea recorded on paper, with no visual to accompany it. I had found the idea fascinating and built upon it, adding layers of detail and gore until it was my masterpiece. I loved the idea, and when the Image first came, I was thrilled to finally be able to see it in a way that writing did not allow. I enjoyed this for some months, and with every word I added, the Image evolved into something grisly. I cannot now grasp why I pursued a thought so disturbing. Maybe the fact that it was so far from reality at the time, so new and unexplored my intellect would not allow for it to go untouched. I think some part of me, or possibly the whole, reveled in the Image day and night because I could not resist the sheer abomination that it was.

That was when it turned from a gruesome fantasy to a parasite. I did not wish to see the Image again. I tried to block it out, to banish it from my thoughts until it was but another dot of a memory to fade with time, but it always resurfaced. I did not know how to rid myself of the Image, the horrid Image, that plagued me just as its idea had what seemed like long ago, but was, in fact, less than a year. After so much time spent in terror, I could not take another moment of the Image. It had opened the door to madness and was attempting to push my now unwilling soul through it. But I would not—will not—go through. The Image will not consume me. Unless it does. But what, then, shall be my course of action? Perhaps I will burn the writing. Yes, that is what started it all, and with its death, the Image shall follow suit.

The sun was high in the cloudless sky, casting its crimson glow upon the landscape. The thick, putrid steam that hung in the atmosphere disturbed vision and burned the lungs. Grass as thick and brittle as a man's stubble protruded from the ground, occasionally producing flowers of vein and skin. The trees consisted of jagged bone that twisted into the firmament. Small grotesque creatures, not identifiable by man but not completely alien either, inhabited these trees, leaving the entrails of their meals to stain the once-white surface. Larger creatures plagued the floor, their disfigured hooves and paws sinking deep into the shredded viscera. There was a muffled squelch that accompanied the footsteps, subtle enough that it could go unnoticed but disturbing enough to pervade the ears and take control of the mind.

A river ran through this place, spilling out into an ocean of blood. Pieces of monsters were violently thrown about in the stream and spat into the outlet. In one scene, a horrid imitation of an ungulate bends to drink from the river, and one of its eyes falls out. It looks up with the remaining two. Its eyes glaze over, wearing an expression of unawareness, as if somewhere in its mind, it has recognized something has gone wrong but could not be bothered to decipher what. Then it walks away and rips up a nearby flower, causing blood to spurt from the exposed artery then dull to a rhythmic pulse. You can, if still enough, feel the soft beating of a heart through your feet. Once found, it flows through you until the beat of yours and this heart become indistinguishable. You can feel yourself mutating, becoming part of this place. The sting of the air becomes pleasurable, the horrid creatures become friends, and the alterations in yourself become miracles.

I hold my carefully worded writing above the flames, staring at the beautiful curves of the letters. The heat in my hand is almost too much as I hesitate. My mind is telling me to release the paper, but my hand will not obey. Indecision holds me in its grasp, battling over the fate of my creation. After some time, the top layer of skin on my hand is seared away leaving an angry, slimy sore in its wake. Still I do not move. Still the Image sits behind my eyes, persuading me to give in. After all, I spent so long on this it would be tragic to destroy it. My arm retracts a few inches, still caught between what I know must be done and what I want to do. I stand there for many more minutes, letting a sharp pain form behind my eyes as they gaze into the shifting brightness. Finally, I have mustered up enough courage to hurl myself into the fire. I watch as my muscles relax around the paper through no will of my own, and a strong gust of heat blows it to safety. The blaze tortures my skin, forcing shrieks from my throat. I am helpless as the flames twist and begin to distort into a river. Panic and terror sweep through me, my hands and feet flailing desperately in an attempt to be free of the inferno. My lungs are burned by smoke then acidic steam as I watch the fire fade away and the Image rise up to greet me.

THE GIRL WITH THE BUTTERFLY WINGS

By Abby Kusmin

August is heavy, like
the weight of the world on our shoulders.
I watched the girl with the butterfly wings
carry it on her back through the streets,
marching past the rivers you bloodied because you
never knew how to stop wanting.
A heat we could not will away pressed forward—
I watched her burn the letters she wrote,
I watched you burn her home down
and learned that all that rises from ashes
is smoke and you cannot rebuild a home from smoke,
let alone a heart.

Even as our lips crack, the oceans break away
the things we used to know.
I watched her disappear into the waves,
too stubborn to be saved.
If we are thankless it is because
we have no air left to thank you for
ripping the wings off our hope.
I watched her as her voice broke
on the last note, singing all she had left that
wouldn't burn.

NAMELESS HERO
(Prologue to a Novel)

By Zafar Mamat

Everything hurt. My chest was swelling, blood pouring out of my gut. My arms were on fire, and my legs were being crushed underneath layers of rubble. I looked to my right and saw a maiden with silk-like white hair dressed in blue. To my horror, blood was pouring out of her, tainting her clothes. An aged voice to my left said, "Whatever you do, you can't change her ending. She will die by your own hands!"

My eyes opened again. I was in a room. A guest tavern with a quiet and constricted space, it seemed. I saw a door to a bathroom on the left, a large table beside my bed with two identical wooden chairs placed beneath it. *Wait, where was I just a moment ago?* The pain was gone. I hurriedly checked my chest. There was no blood. I lifted my vest. There were no wounds. My legs were not injured in the slightest, and my arms didn't reveal signs of burns. Perplexed, I thought to myself, *Who was that girl, and who was that person?*

A knock on the door broke my thoughts. "May I come in?" the voice said.

"Uh, y-yes!" I stuttered.

The door opened, and an elven maid walked into the room. I still couldn't figure out what was going on. *Wait! Why are there elves? Where am I? Is this not…..? Wait, what was the name of the place where I used to live?* "Sir, breakfast will be served until 11. You have ten minutes left. Would you like me to bring your meal up here?"

I couldn't concentrate. *Why an elf?* As I studied her face, it seemed to be quite charming: blonde hair, elegant nose, pointy ears.

"Sir? Are you okay?"

"Huh? Uh, no—I mean yes. I'll go down to breakfast myself," I replied.

She stepped outside and closed the door. *What just happened? I don't remember there being elves in...or, were there elves?* I got up and stood before the large mirror, staring at myself. I was a regular human! Blonde hair, straight nose, toned face, blue eyes, but my pupils surprised me. Unlike a human back on...? *Why couldn't I remember anything?* Suddenly, I noticed my pupils were in the shape of—a diamond? My hair was pretty long, halfway covering my ears and the backside dropping down to my shoulders. I couldn't describe it, but it looked good. I looked at my body. *Hmmm.* I was well toned; I probably had the body of a healthy nineteen-year-old. On the wooden chair lay a sword sheath. It was finely fabricated and superbly stitched. It felt authentic and genuine to the touch. I removed the sheath, exposing a long blade. The metallic blade was glowing. Etched along its surface were strange characters that said "Diablo." *Wait a second. I had never seen those characters in my life, but I could read them.* The sword looked like a katana from...my memory fuzzed out again.

I sheathed the blade and strapped it to my vest. My stomach rumbled. I rushed out the door and down the stairs, almost tripping on my way down. The room where food was being served was massive. I rushed in and grabbed a plate. Large candles floated under the ceiling even though the windows let in plenty of sunlight. The room's occupants were definitely not human. I could identify a few dwarves wearing pointy hats with tools strapped to their waists. There were several elves and dryads sitting near a tree in the right corner of the room. The tree's branches broke through the ceiling, exposing the sunlight. Crystalline panels surrounded the tree, adding additional light. Several fairies and orcs sat at the tables.

"Sir, would you like some food? We are done serving in two minutes," a shimmering man said. "Huh? Um, yes!" I replied, hesitantly. *Was he a ghost?* I stepped up and saw only bread on his counter. It seemed that everyone else had taken all the prepared meals. The ghost man piled a couple of biscuits on my plate along with a small capsule containing a substance that strongly resembled jam. I sat down on a chair in the corner, providing a good view of the entire room. I quickly confirmed that I was in a magical world different from…. *Why can't I remember!?* Frustrated, I munched on my bread, then left the room and ran out of the tavern. I had to explore the area to find some answers.

I ran to the nearby grassland. After a few minutes, I realized that there was no end to the green. I looked back and could see only the tavern, tiny in the distance. Tired, I plopped down onto the grass. I looked closer at my surroundings and saw that the field held not just grass but also flowers. To my left was a large flower bed with pink-petaled flowers packed tightly. As I looked farther beyond, I saw a huge creature resting on a pile of rotten petals. I quietly crept closer to study it. The creature resembled a massive bear. It took me almost a minute to walk from its rear paws to its head. The paws were as large as me, and protruding from its head were three bronze horns. It seemed to be resting peacefully. Not wanting to get involved with the creature, I slowly began walking back to the grassy area. As I was about to step out of the flower bed, I stepped on a stray rock, twisting my ankle and crashing to the ground. The moment I touched the ground, the flowers all flew upwards, creating a beautiful sight.

"RAWRR," the beast growled. The noise of my fall had awoken it. While I liked to imagine myself going head to head with this creature, I ran instead. I didn't know exactly where I was going. My first instinct was to get as far away from that creature as I could.

But the creature was much faster than I. In what seemed like seconds, it trampled me with its huge paw. The fur was quite soft, but the ground was not. Searing pain filled my core. I yelled, "HELP!" I knew, though, that no one could hear me. No one came. My legs were free, but my upper body wasn't. My right hand wouldn't budge underneath the paw. I squirmed, trying to reach my sword with my left arm. The shadow of the creature's face fell upon my face, blocking the sun. His drool dripped down to my face and soon covered my upper body.

I have to get away! I was sure the creature intended to make me its next meal. I finally reached my sheath and struggled to remove the blade. The face of the creature kept coming closer. I thought that I would die there. Suddenly, I heard a *fwoosh!* I opened my eyes as I felt the pressure released from my body. The beast was there, but frozen, its paw no longer holding me down. Suddenly, blood jetted out of its neck, then its head came off and landed a couple feet away from my face. The body crumbled down and disintegrated. All that was left was a golden ore, only as large as a thumb. I looked around to see my savior.

She walked towards me, adjusting her sword sheath. She was wearing a blue vest and a shining white skirt covering her long white socks. I could see her face, with its beautiful complexion, red eyes, white hair. *Ruby eyes, white hair!*

"Whatever you do, you can't change her ending; she will die by your own hands!" The voice repeated itself.

Suddenly, my vision became fuzzy, and before I could thank her, I blacked out. A green light like a levitating circle surrounded by geometrical shapes and particles shone over me. I looked down, avoiding eye contact with the searing bright light, and saw that it was healing the huge scar on my gut. My shirt had been lifted up, but it was stained red. The paw had done more than it seemed.

I was back in my room lying in bed when I saw the elf who had talked to me this morning, eyes closed, focused on casting the circle. Looking left, I saw the woman who saved me reading in a chair. I immediately realized that I was in a room with two young women with my shirt lifted. I blushed in shame.

"Thank y-y-you," I stammered. There was no response. *Was she asleep?* My assumption was right. She had fallen asleep midway through reading. *I'll thank her once she's awake.* The green light disappeared, and the elf opened her eyes once again. "Thank you," I said.

"It's quite alright. Be sure to avoid the pink flower bed. Horn-level demons spawn there frequently," she said, smiling. Sensing that I was staring at her smile, I quickly looked away. Elves were pretty. She left silently and closed the door.

I looked at my gut and saw it had been completely healed. All that was left was a large claw scar. Pulling my shirt down, I looked up at the ceiling covered in art—a painting of three large monsters separated into quadrants. Portrayed were an ice dragon with golden eyes and silver claws and a large wolf with red eyes, pointy ears, and yellow fur covered in sparks. The final painting was a crimson ape dressed in human armor holding a spear covered in skulls. His helmet was in the form of a serpent. Fiery sparks flew from his cape. *Scary!*

"Those are the Three Grand Quests. An adventurer has yet to finish a single quest." Startled, I turned. My savior was awake. She pushed her hair behind her ear as she rose from her seat and came towards me.

"Thank you for saving me. I would have been the creature's breakfast. Thank you."

"Are you feeling well?" she asked.

"Yes. Um, I don't believe I caught your name?" I stammered.

"Isla, Isla Ramilia. And yours?" she asked.

My name? What was my name? I tried to look back in my memories, but all I saw was fuzziness. "I don't know" was all that came out of my mouth. All the pent-up frustration with my memories just came out, "Excuse me, but where am I? I can't remember anything. I don't know my name or where I come from. All I remember is a girl." I said.

Once I finished complaining like a child, I realized that I was crying. Embarrassed with my outburst, I wiped my eyes and covered my face. She seemed genuinely worried, and she moved her chair next to the bed.

"A girl? What do you mean? You didn't finish," she said.

"Whatever you do, you can't change her ending; she will die by your own hands!" The voice repeated itself in my head.

This girl is she. In that case, I can't tell her. "N-Nothing," I replied.

"Well, then, let me answer your questions," she said, smiling.

If she kept smiling, I might come to like her, I thought. Embarrassed, I listened as she explained everything. I tried to process what was going on. We were in the Kingdom of Fyre, one of the twelve kingdoms on the continent of Albatross. Humans, elves, orcs, fairies, and all other beings were under the rule of the king. But another hierarchy existed in power. Humans were very uncommon, as they had been almost entirely wiped out during the second grand quest led by the hero Nux. Those who were just below humans in the power hierarchy were the "special creatures," who supported the humans.

Angels were above humans in the power hierarchy. They blessed a special hero every thousand years, granting the hero the power to harness holy magic. Holy magic varied depending on the user, but in the past, heroes had powers ranging from natural spirit control to control over humans and even to reincarnation.

Demons, meanwhile, came from the underworld and were granted powers by the master much greater than those of angels. The master—or the summoner of the demon—would have to be extremely powerful in order to withstand the demon's memories of tortured souls. Only three successful summons of lesser demons had been accomplished.

Demons and angels had their own class from pawns, footmen, and dukes. Humans were also separated into different roles, ranging from caster, archer, charger, enhancer, thief to knight. The classes of humans were determined based on magical aptitude or the shape of weapon that manifested once the child touched a magical orb. A child had its life planned at that moment. Every one hundred years, only seven humans could use the powers of all the classes. And only one could become a samurai.

Isla explained that the conquerors of the quests could receive any wish they chose. She also explained that she herself was a hybrid, of which there were only a few. A hybrid could harness two classes' powers. She could manifest the powers of an enhancer, being able to enhance her whole body or parts to be more durable and faster, or even enhance herself to receive a longer life span. Her knight class gave her mastery in the long sword and high stamina and royal knight spells. "Do you understand?" she asked.

"I think so. Thank you so much. I owe you a great deal," I replied.

"Sorry, but I still don't know where you have come from. There are too many missing parts in your story. What class are you?" she asked.

Her eyes shone as she looked at my sheath, which was shining now with the blade inside. "I don't know, the blade looked weird to me," I said. Eagerly, like a puppy that just saw a squirrel in an open field, she grabbed the sheath and drew the blade. Her eyes explained it all.

"Y-you're a s-s-samurai?!" she exclaimed. Shocked, I looked at the blade. It was still glowing white.

"But why does it glow? And why does it say 'Diablo'?"

Shocked, she gulped and spoke, "I don't know. Except in pictures, I've never seen a samurai sword before. We have to find out!" She clipped my sheath back onto my vest and grabbed my hand and led me out the tavern.

"Wait! Where are you taking me?"

She ignored the question and led me across the road to a shop. Before she tugged me inside, I caught a small glimpse of the shop's name: Mark's Magical Items. She stopped when we reached the counter in back. The shop's interior seemed aged and crusty. As I looked closer, I could see that the weapons on display were made with high caliber craftsmanship. Magical items and weapons lined the shelves and walls. The shop owner was a bald man with a scar running down from his left eye and a long white beard in curls, neatly tied. He had an intimidating stature. *I do not want to be on his bad side,* I thought.

"Could you give me your sword?" she said after conversing with Mark, the shop owner.

"Huh? Um, Sure. Here," I stammered as I handed her my sword. Mark examined it, studying its markings and holding it up to examine the glow. After a long sigh, he said, "I can only assume that this is the blessing of an angel. But the mark? I can't tell, sorry."

"A blessing of an angel!" we both exclaimed simultaneously.

"Yes. That will be twelve onz," he said.

"Come on, Mark, give me a discount will you?" she begged.

"For such a young maiden, it will be my pleasure. Eleven Onz," he replied.

Grumbling, she took out her pouch, counted the shards, and handed over the payment. Mark put the blade back into the sheath and gave it to me. "Good luck," was all he said.

He didn't seem shocked. I could only assume that this world had gone through so many heroes who had failed that people like Mark had grown accustomed to one appearing. *Had this world lost hope?*

Isla led me out of the shop. She seemed disappointed, but I couldn't understand why. *Did she want to be a hero? But if the world has lost so many. Then, will I die, too?*

"I have a request. I just met you, but you saved my life. If I can be selfish again, could you grant me your aid?" I pleaded.

"Why? Your potential and power are immense. I would only become a burden," she replied.

"It's embarrassing, but, well, I have little knowledge about this world. I would be utterly lost," I said, scratching my head.

"Fine. I'll help you, but I want something in return," she grumbled.

"Huh? You do realize, I have nothing?" I knew she wouldn't budge, however. I would resort to other help if I could, but I didn't know anyone else. *Ah, yes, that's it. I don't have a name do I? Hmm.*

"Why don't you choose my name," I said.

She stood there for a second, then she grinned and said, "How about ...?"

"Huh? I didn't catch that. What did you say?" I asked. Once again, she smiled.

"Whatever you do, you can't change her ending. She will die by your own hands!" The voice repeated itself in my mind. *I don't know anything about her or about my role in this world, but something tells me I have to conserve that smile as long as I can. Whatever it takes.*

QUARANTINE THOUGHTS

By Fatimah Iqbal

I've yet to process what's happened. So quickly, we were ushered into our homes. I don't think I even said goodbye to half of my friends. It's certainly not the same over text. I haven't gotten a full moment to myself since quarantine began. My entire family's on one floor because our basement, with perfect timing, flooded the day before quarantine was enacted.

My sister has taken over my room, so I have no land to claim as my own. I'm either sharing a bed or sleeping on a couch, and no matter how many windows I open, the room stubbornly remains suffocatingly hot. I get kicked out of my own room countless times. Take my friend Gillian's word for it, she's witnessed it from the other end of FaceTime.

I don't really become active or alive until 1 or 2 a.m., which is unfortunate. Every member of my family—including me—spends entire mornings and afternoons switching rooms aimlessly while on our phones. My hobbies now are taking showers, eating, and waiting for it to get dark so I can sleep.

Sometimes, the anxiety and realization of what's happening around the world gets to me. How are my friends and their families being affected? Stepping outside, I see people with masks on and posters about social distancing. It feels surreal. There is no life in Potomac; no one smiles now; people step back when you step forward. It's straight out of a Stephen King novel.

As for school, it's concerning how much I don't care about it. Goofing off in class isn't the same anymore. The only way to pass a note to your friend is to write it in a public chat shared with the whole class. I still find it baffling that we're even having school. In Potomac and around the world, people are getting infected with the coronavirus and dying. We're using terms like "social distancing" and "exposure" like we're in a dystopian novel. Do you really think that's not going to have a toll on a student's mental health? *I'm sorry, Mr. Ho, I didn't do my weekly check-in worth six points. I was too busy staring at the wall for three hours contemplating if life is real.*

I have a year left of high school and a full bucket list of hijinks I need to complete to be satisfied with how I've spent my teen years. Getting arrested for one, either from a protest or trespassing on government property; I haven't quite decided yet. But now that I am confined to my home, I feel so helpless. I feel my teen years pass by, day by day, while I am locked in from the rest of the world. A police arrest, maybe, but house arrest was never in the plan.

As much as I miss the opportunity to do something outrageous, I miss the mundane. I hope that when we get out of this situation, hopefully safely, we'll appreciate things like going out to eat or hugging someone. It's funny, you never know how much you miss something until it's made illegal.

FATE

By Sydney Wu

"Fate isn't set in stone,"
says the savior,
"we can all change it together."
The heads nod as he raises his eyes.

"Fate isn't set in stone,"
he looks at all of them,
"we can all heal together."
He smiles.

"What was lost is now found."
He encircles them in a hug.
"Whatever happens we have each other!"
They hug back.

"Fate isn't set in stone,"
he looks them all in the eyes,
"even past actions aren't."
Their eyes widen.

"The past doesn't affect the future,"
he assures them,
"we can put it all behind us."
Their smiles join his.

"We can all be together,
not fight separate battles.
We can heal together."
They all agree.

"Fate isn't set in stone—
we will change our fates together
and forever we will live
no longer tormented or afraid!"

"All together, we can do anything."

STRANGERS
(Beginning of a Novel)

By Nicole Hawks

Avery jolted awake and felt a sharp pain in his gut. He tried to shake off the haze of sleep and a dream he barely remembered, although it took him some time. He eventually became aware enough of his surroundings that he realized he was in an unrecognizable room.

The room was dimly lit by a half-melted candle. It was big enough for him to walk around, but it was still small. There were no windows or vents that he could see. He was on top of a bundle of blankets serving as a mildly uncomfortable, makeshift bed.

Avery decided to try and get up, but his legs shook, and he fell down. The pain in his stomach doubled in intensity, and now he probably had skinned kneecaps to boot.

He curled back up in an attempt to try and go back to sleep. He was greeted with more pain when he moved. He still refused to look at the injury. He was afraid of what he would find.

He really hated blood and the like, and he knew that looking at the injury would scare him more. He had enough to worry about without thinking of bleeding out.

Avery heard the door creak open, and he faced away from it. He hoped that his unwelcome visitors would just pass by him if he pretended to sleep.

"Still sleeping," a voice said. Avery could hear someone walking over, the sound of footsteps far too close for comfort.

"Give the boy time. He's badly hurt," another said. The

footsteps continued again, and Avery assumed whoever approached him was walking away now.

"He's been asleep for two days, Angel."

Avery opened his eyes and shifted a little to get a better look. A large woman with long purple hair, who Avery guessed was Angel, came over towards him.

"You're finally awake," she said and crouched down to look at him. "How do you feel?"

Avery made a faint squeaking noise in response that was intended to be a word. She was far too close for comfort.

"Hey, it's okay," Angel said and backed away. "You're safe here. What's your name?"

"Avery." He spoke slowly and carefully. His voice sounded almost unnatural. It seemed deeper and scratchy, but he assumed it was just because of dehydration. He didn't really care, though; if he was cooperative, maybe Angel would be nice.

A blond boy whose voice Avery assumed was the first he'd heard watched him carefully with one violet eye. A chill ran down Avery's spine.

"Okay, Avery. I'm Angel, and that boy there is Esther." Angel turned over to Esther. "Come here and say hi."

Esther uncrossed his arms and walked to them. He bent down to look at Avery and tilted his head to the side. "Hey. Roll over."

Angel looked confused by the request. "Esther?"

"Trust me, Angel."

Avery hesitated but rolled over. Esther didn't seem like a person to cross, so he would have to be careful. It hurt but he didn't want to upset the two strangers at all.

"Your wings are gone," Angel said, sounding shocked.

"Wings?" Avery rolled back over, this time letting out a pained hiss. He looked up at the two with wide blue eyes.

"What wings?"

Esther made a face, and Avery feared that he would start getting mad. But he sighed and glanced over at Angel.

"You had them when we found you in the snow," Angel explained softly. It reminded Avery of what he remembered of his mother. "Do you know how you got there? How did you get stabbed?"

"I don't know," Avery said. His voice shook. He didn't remember falling asleep in the snow. He fell asleep in an alleyway, and the only pain he had felt was hunger.

But what were you doing there? A voice hissed. It sounded like his, but it was different. It brought a low ringing sound with it and it reminded Avery of a snake.

He shook his head and tried to keep calm. He'd always had a tendency to get riled up fast, and the voice was surely just a product of that. "I didn't fall asleep in the snow. I don't know how I got stabbed. It wasn't even that cold when I fell asleep!"

Angel stayed quiet for a while with a concerned and almost frightened expression. She shared a look with Esther, who rose to his feet. Avery wondered when he had started kneeling.

"Where did you fall asleep?" Angel asked.

"In an alleyway. In Dian." Avery shifted uncomfortably.

"In Dian?" Esther echoed. He sounded surprised.

Avery nodded. "I think so."

"Dian's miles and miles from here," Esther said. He squinted. "We're on the outer ring, near Bossen. How did you wind up here?"

Avery balled his hands into fists and avoided looking at Esther. "I don't know." Nothing made sense to him at this point. He tried to pull his knees as close to his chest as he could without making his gut hurt any more than it

58   Emerging Voices already did. Maybe that was why he was so panicky.

Angel frowned and placed a hand on Avery's leg. He flinched, and she removed it. "Hey, don't worry. You're okay. We'll help you figure this out." Her eyes drifted to his injury, and he looked up at the ceiling. Now that he knew what it was, he was even more afraid of looking at it.

"Let's get these bandages replaced first, though. Esther, could you watch Avery while I go get more supplies?"

Esther nodded and crouched beside Avery. He watched Angel leave the room, and Avery could see sharp canines poking out of his mouth.

It was quiet for a while. Neither of them seemed to know what to say.

"What are you?" Esther asked. His voice was lower than before, and he almost glared at Avery.

The boy watched the door for any signs of Angel. "Human."

"Humans don't have wings." Esther scowled. "And they can't lose them, even if they do have them."

"I didn't have them when I fell asleep." Avery hid his face. Esther terrified him. He was too much like his caretakers in the past and the scornful people who passed him on the street.

Esther relaxed. "You don't know what happened? You really don't?" He shook his head. "I may have an idea."

Avery stayed silent.

"Angel's a witch. She's been trying to show me signs of possession."

"What?"

"Gaps in your memory, growing body parts to fit the spiritual form of what possessed you." Esther sat down beside Avery. "Think. Can you remember anything from when you were asleep?"

Poetry and Prose by Maryland Teens

Avery still stayed silent. Esther was starting to grow more eerie than terrifying, now, which scared Avery more. He didn't know what Esther was talking about, and he didn't want to know.

Angel entered the room before Esther could pry any further. She smiled when she saw the two boys sitting next to each other, and she kneeled beside Avery.

"Glad to see you two are getting along," she said as she began to undo Avery's bandages.

It seemed like hours before Angel had finished. Esther watched them the entire time.

"Done!" she said. "That was easy, wasn't it? Are you hungry?"

Avery shook his head. "Tired."

Angel gave him a kind look. "Alright. We'll leave you be, then. Come on, Esther." She grabbed her gear and rose to her feet. She motioned for Esther to follow her as she left.

"Think about it," Esther said to Avery. "We can help each other out." His eye seemed to shine like a cat's. "Don't be difficult."

As he shut the door, Avery decided that he wouldn't think about it. He curled up in his makeshift bed and tried to shut out thoughts of the snow. Being cooperative was no longer a priority for him as far as Esther was concerned.

Interesting.

PANDEMIC

By Siya Behl

Trapped in a house with only one door
a couple of windows and three small floors

filled with emotions we can't understand
surrounded by the same people which wasn't quite
    planned

worrying over things which never crossed our minds
trying to protect ourselves from contact of all kinds

released from daily duties to be burdened by more
don't know how long we can keep it outside the door

BELOW
(Beginning of a Novel)

By Gillian Wesson

Mist curls around the roots of ancient oaks. Thick moss and lichen coat the ground, surrounding vast clumps and thickets of fern and bramble. The monolithic trees spiral upwards, their foliage so dense that all sunlight is blocked, as if the whole forest is deep underwater. Birdsong echoes from afar, but none originates from this grove. Seldom ever does a fox or deer wander here. The glade harbors a small pond with dark water that is still and lifeless, a pool of black glass. The glade is so deep into the forest that no wind has grazed the surface of the pond for a long time. A single lily pad lies in the pond, close to the shore. Atop the lily pad, a blossom of a startling crimson hue grows. The roots of the lily pad extend deep below, far deeper than they could normally grow.

Leah takes it all in—this beautiful, ancient treasure. The forest is even more enchanting than she once imagined. All insecurity and uncertainty had subsided upon arrival. The idea of coming here had popped into her head one day, and after it had come to mind, it had nagged at her for months and months, disturbing her thoughts. That incessant cycle of thought had been almost maddening. So, yesterday, she had decided to put an end to it and take a trip to the forest.

Soft chatter comes from the group as the guide describes a rare lichen species. Leah half listens, her mind wandering. Suddenly, she feels a pull within her. It is almost like the forest is beckoning to her, urging her onward. She leaves the group and walks up a steep slope and across a creek, following the pull. The forest seethes with life. She walks on, eager and curious. Life flourishes all around her—ancient trees, birds, flowers, deer. The forest is alive and bright, with a seemingly boundless energy. She gazes in wonder as she walks onward.

Leah loses track of time, stopping only when she is deep into the woods. It is dark. She realizes hours must have elapsed. She feels the pull; it tugs at her, persistent. She checks her watch and looks up, confused. It shouldn't be dark yet; it is only noon. Still, it has been hours since she has seen the group. She does not have a single clue as to how to get back. Panic wells in her chest, but curiously fades, as if the feeling is being suffocated. She turns and looks down the path, which has shifted from well-worn to almost nonexistent. The depths of the forest call, and she answers. Her hand falls to her side and she continues forward, diverging from the path. It grows darker and quieter as she forges ahead, pushing aside brambles and thorny bushes with an almost frantic energy, failing to notice that her hands are covered in cuts.

The pull grows stronger, pounding within her chest like a second heartbeat, fast and heavy. Her breathing quickens and she breaks into a run, delving into the undergrowth. She stumbles into a secluded glade, so dimly lit that it could be midnight. The pull strengthens its grip, drawing her forward. In the center of the grove, a pool of dark water lies still. She hesitantly takes one step, and another, and another, and stops at the edge of the water.

There is a single lily in the pond, a lily with blood-red petals. She drops to her knees, craning her neck at the lily. The pull threatens to envelop her in darkness, the loud beats pounding inside her skull. As she approaches the lily, it begins to glow a stronger and more violent crimson. She leans forward, nearly falling into the motionless water, reaching out toward the flower. In the moment before she touches it, the last rational part of her mind urges her to flee. But her better instincts fade away under the pull, swept into the dark current.

Her finger touches the edge of the longest petal, and the pull vanishes. Silence overtakes the glade. The flower withers, the petals browning and falling into the water, its red glow waning into nothingness, and the glade once again grows dark. Leah pulls back her hand, dazed. Her instincts return to her, begging her to run. Fear and confusion bloom in her mind. She tries to stand.

The glade darkens, lit only by the lily's sickly blood-red glow. Desperate to flee but unable to move, Leah can only watch. Her eyes turn to the water, dark and murky yet no longer still. In that moment, deep within her mind, she remembers that the water did not ripple when the lily petals fell in. A single ripple breaks the surface, flowing across the pond, and then once again is still. As she gazes into the depths, terror seizes her racing heart as two pinpricks of red light burn below. The pull seizes her once again, but this time, it does not take away her fear.

MIDNIGHT BEND

By Abby Kusmin

Maybe she was the one you wanted
and lost, the one with her
tongue bitten bloody
between her teeth, iron filling her mouth,
not letting the regret
spill out over her lips onto
the white dress you gave her that
barely fit anymore.

Maybe she didn't hear you say goodbye
because her ears were full of lilies,
music, or the cry of someone who
loved her once and still.

Maybe it was the faded stars and spider
veins all the way down your legs—
the proof that you couldn't sit
still without looking up towards the
sky, and how, on nights when it was cloudy, you would
invent your own constellations,
make the midnight bend toward you
and take it in your arms, whisper how you
loved it.

Maybe she remembers you from a dream she had
once, where her hair was red and her
fingers bled onto the pages you had filled with
words you had written just to have written
them, or maybe it was the one where she
woke to a red dawn with a stranger's eyes
and a lake in her chest.

Maybe she will sit on the docks and wait
for you until sunset, when the wind
whispers go home,
or maybe she will leave at the break
of noon, when the sun is high and the sweat
on her back reminds her there is another way
to be alive.

GET OUT

By Fatimah Iqbal

My eyes stayed shut, but I knew I was back in reality because the flashes of eating sticky sweet orange chicken from Panda Express had halted. My body ached like I had been run over by one of those neon-blue Ride On buses then had a hundred-pound refrigerator placed on my chest. The linen hospital blankets did little to bring me warmth, the AC blew a never ending chill onto my chest and arms. I heard the door creak open, and I held my breath, keeping my eyes closed. I could hear someone calling to me softly from a couple of feet away. "Alma... Alma." It sounded muffled, like their mouth was covered. I froze. This didn't sound like a doctor—more like someone my age. I tried my best to lie still and appear unconscious. I assumed they gave up when I heard the door's heavy thump as it creaked shut and I opened my eyes. The dreary room did little to ease my anxieties, with its sickening seafoam colored walls and the only light coming through the window, outside of which was a desolate city. I turned my head to the door, wondering who had been beckoning me a couple of seconds ago. An IV was connected to my left arm, and machines surrounded the bed.

The door opened again, and my heart raced. Was it the mystery visitor? A nurse walked in wearing a mask. She had bags under her eyes, and hair fell from her bun, wisps surrounding her face. Still, I could see from her eyes that she was mustering a smile. She said she was glad to see me awake. I tried to ask her how long I had been unconscious, but only a hoarse squeak came from my throat.

"Oh, sweetie, your throat won't work right away. Write what you need on this notepad," she said, pulling a notepad and pen the size of my palm out from under her nurse's gown. I scribbled, "How long was I out for?" I showed it to her. She smiled and replied, "Only for about two days, though it's not uncommon for patients to slip in and out right after waking up. You may experience hallucinations. It's normal."

Two days? But I could've sworn I'd woken up from this coma countless times, countless nights. Wasn't there a ventilator machine hooked up to me? Where did that go? Has the coma distorted my reality this much?

She smiled before her eyes moved to my left arm, which I thought had the IV line in it. "Look what's fallen out, again," she muttered to herself, reaching over to my arm. She plucked the needle off the side of the bed, a sight I had clearly missed, before sharply sticking it back in the tube connected to my arm. I felt a sting and then a cold feeling in my veins.

"Have you been taking this out?" Her tone had dropped. I shook my head. *How could I if I had been unconscious?* She stared at me unconvinced as she handed me pills in a small plastic cup and another cup filled with water. I quickly forgot about the strange exchange. I was just relieved to have water. My throat felt spiky as I swallowed the pills and then the water, but I was glad to get something to soothe myself. I laid back down, placing the notepad on the table next to me. I felt nauseated, and my eyes were pulled shut by the sleepiness; I felt myself slipping into a dream, my mind too exhausted to wake itself.

I started to feel as if I were spinning and being tossed around in space. I began to see stars and flashes of purple and blue swirls. It was beautiful, but it also unsettled me; I feared I was falling back into a coma again. It must've been a couple of hours before I was jolted awake. I couldn't describe the feeling. I knew someone was in my room. My eyes weren't adjusted to the darkness in the hospital room, but I could feel the presence of someone. It wasn't pitch black, but somehow worse. The faint lights from the signs and street lamps outside made it virtually impossible for me to make out objects in the room.

My vision slowly adjusted to the blackness, though objects still seemed distorted as I looked around the room. I began to identify objects to ease my mind—the chair, the IV, the monitors, the framed prints, the TV in the corner, the cabinet, the coat hanger. *No, coat hangers don't crouch over cabinets.* My heart sank. Without moving my head or neck out of fear of making a single noise that signified I was awake, I shifted my eyes to the right. The door was cracked open. Not wide, but wide enough for someone to suck in their gut and squeeze through. I heard shuffling. *Who is that?* I looked in front of me. The figure was quietly opening cabinets, looking through medications, reading the labels on the small orange plastic containers before taking them. Was this a patient desperate for medication? Was this even real? I was paralyzed with fear.

The figure turned around. I shut my eyes, trying to level my breathing. I could feel the air shift as the figure made its way to the side table at my right. I held my breath. They picked something up. I heard a soft noise I couldn't figure out. The person paused. Were they looking at me? I stayed still, though inside I was fighting the urge to start bawling out of fear. I felt slow movements in front of me. The person was reaching across my chest. I felt a tug on my arm—no, something in my arm. The IV needle. It was being pulled out. I struggled to keep my act together as my body felt like I was melded with the hospital bed, powerless to this torment. My palms were sweating as I fought to control my facial muscles from moving. Sharp pain shot up my arm as the needle was tucked under my blanket so as to look as if it was still in. The figure made its way back to the door, squeezing through the gap without making a sound. I opened my eyes slightly, trying to catch a glimpse of this freak. All I could make out was long brown hair and a purple cardigan. It couldn't have been a patient or a nurse, so who was it?

I didn't sleep the entire night. I was afraid to put the IV back in. It was so dark I probably would have stabbed myself in the wrong place. But I felt more alert. I used this energy to glue my eyes to the rectangular window in the door. I didn't know who this person was or if they'd be paying me a visit again tonight.

As the sun rose, the hospital sounds became louder and louder. The door to my room was still ajar. I could hear every squeak of the staff's rubber-soled shoes and sneakers as they rushed by, tending to patients and talking amongst themselves. Suddenly, the nurse and doctor stopped outside my door. They talked in low voices, but it was clear they were frantic from the way their heads moved and their eyes shifted. Because of their masks, their voices were muffled and I couldn't read their lips. I thought, *Oh god, could this be about my infection? Is it escalating?* Horrible images flashed in my mind of being hooked up to the ventilator again. Though I could never prove I was hooked up to one, I seriously believed I had been at some point. You don't just make up the feeling of dry air being forcefully pumped into your lungs.

But the only thing escalating for now was this

conversation between the doctor and nurse. The nurse was getting worked up. I picked up some words, though they clarified nothing. "I told you from the beginning... last night...snuck...every room...patients...suspect... public find out...scandal."

Then it was the doctor's turn to talk. He dropped his voice lower so it was even harder to pick up. All I managed to make out was: "taken care of...catatonic...now... continue normal."

The doctor put his hand on the nurse's shoulder before swiftly moving past her, and the nurse opened the door and walked in, tears in her eyes. I quickly changed my demeanor to make it seem as if I were observing my hospital gown even as I tried to comprehend what I had picked up. The nurse asked me how I had slept and if I was feeling better, but I could tell she was distracted. She scanned the room as if she too knew someone had been here. As she walked to my cabinet and looked through my medications, I reached to my side and picked up the notepad and pen to inform her of the stolen bottles and the odd occurrences that happened last night.

The nurse turned around and in a shaky voice said, "I'm going to go grab your medication quickly...it seems to be misplaced because of some...incidents that have occurred around the hospital...but the hospital cares for the safety of our patients, and we've taken care of the situation."

She looked like she was about to throw up. Her words seemed to come straight from a script that she was no doubt being forced to mouth. She stepped out of the room, shut the door, and locked it. I looked down at the notepad, trying to flip to a clean page so I could tell the nurse what I'd witnessed. But the next page was full, full of words I didn't write. Suddenly, the unknown noise I had heard over my bed became clear. It was scribbling. I gulped before squinting my eyes to make out the shaky handwriting:

They're lying to you. It's been months. They're testing on you. They won't find a cure. Their trials are horrifying. Don't become another failed subject. I'm going to tell everyone. Don't take the pills. Don't eat the food. Fight the sleep. GET OUT.

I heard the door jiggle, and I shoved the notepad into my pillowcase. The nurse was back with a tray that held a plate of some meat in a dark sauce with a scoop of mashed potatoes and a glass of milk. She set the tray down along with a cup of pills and a cup of water. I sprang up before she could see my IV was out.

"Ring when you're done, sweetie, and please finish it off. Your health depends on it," she said, then turned around, quickly walked out, and locked the door once again.

I stared at the tray, feeling sick and disturbed. I looked at the food closely; there were remnants of some powder alongside the rim of the glass and around the mashed potatoes. This hit me harder than those Ride On buses ever could. I scooped the pills into my palm and shoved them into my pillowcase. I felt around the case to get an idea of how many of my belongings I could fit into it. I felt like hell, but tonight I needed to listen to my gut and take the advice of whoever left that note. I needed to get the hell out.

A FOREST CORRUPTED

By Sydney Wu

Blood drips upon ruined stone
red moss spreading on the surface
the trees droop and weep
sad for the losses of all

the flowers shrivel and die
making way for thorns to grow
bare tree roots pierce
the bodies of the dead

once a forest of magic and light
now is a forest of evil and dark
corrupted by the blood of men
and by their bodies it has grown

forest no longer
now Death's playground
and may he play
now and forever

WIDOW

By Anna Etienne

He sinks under the suffocating smoke,
his large dark silhouette bent towards his doom.
He collapses under the cloud of smoke,
smothered by murderous hands.
His potent breath is forever silenced,
marked by a burning cross on his front lawn.
His wife watches his cross engulfed in flames,
smoke burning in her eyes, she falls to her knees.
Now his body is hung like a trophy—
magnolia petals flow down on him
emitting the sweet, citrus smell of summer beginning
as life is ending.
His corpse is overwhelmed by the flames licking at his
    feet.
Blood flows from the petals
into the hands of his murderers.
The church choir sings as they wash away his blood,
the end of their song marked by bullets raining from a
    long gun.
In the southern magnolias, other bodies are hanging,
swaying in the summer breeze.

SHELVED

By Fatimah Iqbal

February 15, 1975

The bell jingled as Louis Reeves opened the door to enter the store, and sharp cold air briefly interrupted Bedrock Flames' warm atmosphere. Every inch of the store's walls was lined with candles, illuminating the place with a purple and green hue and filling the room with an aroma of scents. Fleetwood Mac played through the speakers. Although the shop was usually frequented by elders looking to stock up on gifts for any occasion, many teens were attracted to the store to cover up their tobacco scent. The store was crowded that day, and Louis entered the same way he always did: his head down, hands in his pockets, avoiding any contact with the customers as he made his way to the security of the back office. This was less of a job to him than more of a place where Louis sought escape from his claustrophobic apartment.

Home wasn't a place of comfort or entertainment for Louis, but a place to silently return for lukewarm leftovers. It was a place to lie in bed, ignoring the tornado of thoughts that haunted him—thoughts of women, thoughts of holding hands, kissing, flirting, feeling euphoric for a couple of months—then returning home to an empty closet and missing suitcases. He owned neither a TV nor a radio. Anything the TV showed or the artists on the radio sang about focused on the one thing that plagued his mind: love. He owned a small selection of books—books in which the main character was typically stranded on an island or trapped in a cave. He empathized with the main character's feelings of hopelessness and entrapment. He knew what it was like. He lay in his bed, trying to push his anxieties to the far corners of his mind. But the corners were never far enough, and the guilt would creep up within him. The guilt that his parents would be deprived of grandchildren would send him into fits of shallow breaths. They would be deprived because any woman who looked into his eyes saw nothing but a pathetic soul.

Bedrock Flames was his distraction. Now that the holiday he dreaded the most was over and the store was back to its usual bohemian setting, he could finally return. He had called in sick for the week to avoid sitting in a personal hell for hours every day. Valentine's Day couldn't have gone sooner. He sat in the far back room in a torn-up leather chair boxing candles for delivery. It was close to 9 p.m. He was closing up tonight. The backroom door squeaked open, and Louis looked up to see the warm wrinkled face and silver haired Sonny, who always wished him a farewell before heading to his beat-up turquoise Dodge van. Louis's relationship with the cashier was peculiar. Sonny would share stories from fighting in Korea to marching on Washington, and Louis would awkwardly nod, lacking any riveting stories of his own life to share. Nevertheless, Louis enjoyed his company.

"I'm heading out ol' cat; shop's closed and locked." His bead necklaces swayed back and forth as he spoke, clinking against the steel door.

Louis gave a polite smile, and Sonny threw a peace sign in return, his kind eyes twinkling as if to say *Look out for yourself kid*. Then he was gone, the steel door slowly swinging closed. Louis stared at the door for a couple of seconds, as if expecting Sonny to come back, before returning to his work.

In his own bubble, he didn't think— he couldn't think— over the erratic sounds of the nearby malfunctioning heater, the wind howling outside as snow built up rapidly, the candles' jars clinking, and the sound of ripping tape— zzzrrrpttt, zzzrrrpttt, zzzrrrpttt! The tape kept Louis sane, interrupting his anxious thoughts, soothing his anxiety.

Louis had finished boxing, but as he yanked the tape from the dispenser, only a short stub came off. It was empty. He needed a new roll. He sighed, then made his way to the supply closet down the hall. One piece of tape stood between him and trudging home to eat a bowl of stale Cheerios for dinner. Lost in his thoughts of whether the milk in the fridge had expired, he pushed open the heavy door. It was dark, but he knew the shelf closest to him usually had the big rolls of packaging tape. Sticking one foot in the door, he stepped, blindly running his hands over the shelf, hoping to grasp anything shaped like a roll of tape. He stretched farther, struggling to keep his foot planted as he reached farther and farther. His ankle gave out, his body crashed down, and the door slammed shut. After a few heavy deep breaths and hoping, praying the door wasn't locked, he stood up, legs shaking as he felt around for the door handle. When he grasped the cold metal, he took a deep breath and pulled. It didn't move. No, no, no, he whispered to himself, desperately yanking the handle. It didn't budge. He moved his hand along the door then to the wall, looking for a light switch. Feeling the toggle, he flipped it, though the flickering white fluorescent light didn't make him feel better. He turned around to assess his surroundings, his heart palpating as a feeling of horror enveloped him. There were hearts. There were pink and red balloons. There were cards with big white cursive letters and teddy bears holding hearts and dead roses and streamers. The smell of factory chocolate full of chemicals began to enter his nose as his eyes followed the scent to a shelf of stacked boxes of the unsold sweets.

Every alarm bell in his head rang. Every trigger was triggered. Louis lost control. He snapped and started slamming his hands against the door. Gathering all the air in his lungs, he screeched at a deafening volume, "HELP! HELLO, PLEASE, ANYONE! PLEASE! OH GOD, PLEASE HELP! HELP ME! HELP ME!"

With every slam, his face was getting hotter and hotter as tears ran down it. He slammed the door with his hands, his palms getting redder and redder. He stopped for a second to hear anything, keys jingling or hurried footsteps, anything that was a sign he'd get out of there. Silence. He let out a sob as he slid down, facing away from the door, pressing his knees into his eyes.

He peeked at his watch. It was 10:03 p.m. He cautiously glanced around. His heart started to race again as he saw the posters on the floor. The top one showed a handsome, clean-cut, dark-haired man being hugged by a blonde woman holding a candle, and the writing below said, "The Perfect Gift!" The poster made him nauseated as his brain forced him to picture himself as the man, having to feel her hugging him tighter and tighter. He banged his head against the door to snap out of it. Shutting his eyes, he realized the chocolate smell was getting hard to ignore, so he breathed through his mouth instead.

To clear his mind, he thought of an empty open box and twenty candles off to the side ready for shipment. He imagined picking up the candles and placing them into the box. That's it; he was boxing. That's all he was doing.

He took some candles, placed them into the box and then picked up and packed more and more until the boxes and candles disappeared, until his thoughts became a black void and his consciousness slipped away.

February 16, 1975

When Louis's eyes opened, his surroundings were still the same, except one of the pink streamers had fallen from the shelf onto his legs. He kicked it away. His anxiety started to rise again. He was still trapped. He checked his watch: 5:24 a.m. Oh my god, thank the lord, he thought, almost chuckling out of insanity. Only two more hours, you can do it, he told himself. In two hours, she was going to open the door and find him there. He would rush out, no explanation, to home. His apartment seemed to offer immense rapture. Rapture from this horror he had endured, being closed in from every wall with objects that induced such paralyzing fear within him—that had such control over him. *Two more hours, Louis,* he whispered, closing his eyes again.

Outside the closet and outside Bedrock, Camila, the cashier and owner, trudged through the snow. It was up to three-and-a-half feet now, and the weathermen predicted more. Once she reached the door, she pulled a small sign from her bag that she had made with the cardboard insert from one of her husband's laundered shirts. She placed the sign on the door:

*Closed until further notice
due to severe weather conditions.
Sorry for any inconvenience.*

She taped it securely so the wind wouldn't blow it away. With a sigh of relief that it stayed up, she turned and made her way back home.

TALISMAN

By Fiona McKee

In the lake reflected hangs the silent moon,
a stately crescent still as silence,
silvery as cloudless night.
Across the plane in timeless peace a ripple glides,
the crystal reflection undulates.
Sleep reigns yet as the world is still.
A whisper shouts, and a cold breeze blows.
Serenity shatters like glass—
the silver crescent is no longer,
the talisman of peace fractured.
For an instant illusion again reigns,
serenity returns for a heartbeat.
Appearing again the reflection darkens,
hands of fog are all that show,
shadowy clouds drowning the ethereal light.
The moon trembles, holding its breath.
A thunderous roar rends peace to shards,
wind like a mad horse tears the water to froth and foam.
Wet droplets lash down from boiling clouds above,
bursting into oblivion as they hit,
lost in the turmoil of the racing lake.
In the water reflected no more
is the talisman of peace.

A BUMP IN THE NIGHT

By Gillian Wesson

Thud.

My eyes snapped open as the sound woke me. I rolled over, groaning at the time on my digital clock: 2:07 a.m. The quiet sounds of the gentle pitter patter of rain on the window were disrupted by my dog's sudden barking. Maple bounded over to my door and dug at the floorboards.

"Mmrph. Maple, go to sleep." My voice was gravelly, and my mouth tasted sour. "Blech," I grunted, groping for the glass on my bedside table. The water was cool as it slipped slowly down my throat. I sat up, disgruntled and bleary. It was Saturday morning. My Saturday would now be plagued with exhaustion and the grumps, as my mother referred to them. But she wasn't here now; both of my parents were out of town visiting Aunt Lola in Richmond. I screwed up my eyes and rubbed them with balled fists, feeling sorry for myself. A pleasant morning of videogames and Froot Loops™ ruined.

Thud.

My pity party was abruptly interrupted by whatever was making those noises. I paused mid-eye rub and looked around. Maple was still scratching at the bottom of the door, emitting the occasional whine of urgency. I stood up groggily and opened the door for her. She loped down the hallway, claws clicking on the hardwood. Home alone, concern stirred in my chest.

I didn't hear any footsteps, but I did hear a thud. Two

thuds, to be precise. Not normal at this hour.

I flexed my feet into the carpet, feeling the wiry filaments between my toes. My face grew hot, and my breath quickened. I snatched up my phone, fumbling for the home button. I mashed it in a state of semi-panic, incorrectly typing in my passcode before finally getting it correct and unlocking it. Pressing the phone app, I selected my mom's number. I listened to the ring—one, two, three rings before I heard her voice message. "Hi, you've reached Laura Beckett, please leave a message!" Beep. Feeling the first beads of sweat on my upper lip, I tried my dad. Nothing. Straight to voicemail.

"Shoot!" I whispered, ending the call. I pocketed my phone in my pajama pants with now-quivering hands. I covered my face with my palms, forcing myself to take deep breaths. Outside, the wind picked up, and the once gentle rainfall stirred into a storm. *Should I call 911?* I thought anxiously. *But it's a crime to put in a false call. I don't want to be arrested!* My mind whirled as I tried valiantly to control my breathing. *What's worse: being murdered in my bedroom or being arrested? I'll take the latter, please and thank you.* Steeling my resolve, I dialed the three scariest numbers in the world on my iPhone's keypad.

"Nine-one-one, what's your emergency?" A stern female voice answered. In my addled state of mind, I mused that she sounded a bit like Aunt Lola.

"Um...Hi." I fell into a nervous silence for several excruciating seconds. *Idiot! Say something!*

"This line is only for emergencies. It is a crime to use nine-one-one for nonemergencies. If there's no emergency, hang up." I heard a note of annoyance in her tone, and my nerves of steel corroded.

"No. Wait! Sorry, I'm just really nervous." There was an

audible shake in my voice, but I didn't care about that right now. "I'm home alone, and I heard noises in my house." My lip quivered as I wiped at my moistened eyes.

"Give me your address."

"Yeah… It's, uh, 80724 Garnet Lane. Please hurry." My voice was more like a whimper now, and my legs had turned to Jell-O.

"Help is on the way. Please stay on the li…" Click. Dead silence on the line. I pulled my phone away from my ear. The call had ended. In the top left-hand corner of my screen, it read: NO SERVICE. My mind went to the storm that was picking up outside. *Maybe it knocked down a cell phone antenna or something,* I thought, as my semi-panic morphed into full-fledged panic.

Thud.

My eyes shot over to my open bedroom door. My eyes had adjusted to the dark, and the empty, midnight blue hallway was far from comforting.

"Hello? Hello!" I spat into my phone. My voice rose to a comically loud stage whisper, which I would have found funny if I had not been in my current situation. "Ok," I said aloud, dropping onto my bed and rubbing my hands on my pajama pants. "Ok." *What do I do now? Had they even sent anyone? Ok, breathe. Breathe. You need a plan of action.* I ran through possibilities in my head. Jump out of the window and make a break for it until I get to the Harrisons' house? It was a long walk; we lived in a pretty rural neighborhood with a lot of space between the houses. I looked at my bare feet, then I looked out the window at the roaring wind and rain. *Maybe not. Scratch that.* I thought about the other option: Go downstairs and take my chances to try to escape out the front door. I peered down the hall. *Definitely not.*

Jumping out the window it is.

Thud. Thud.

No time for indecision.

I cracked open the window, the sounds of the downpour flooding in. I shivered as the icy rain stung my face. I pushed up the frame and swung one leg out. I gripped the windowsill with all my might and peered down. *It's not that far. You'll be fine. Give or take.* I sucked in a breath of cold air and breathed out slowly. I swung out my other leg and prepared to jump.

Maple.

The realization hit me like a freight train. *I can't leave without her,* I thought guiltily. I climbed back inside and shut the window. Staring into the dark hallway, I gripped my phone in my sweaty palms.

Ok. I started to walk down the hall, cautious and quiet. "Maple," I whispered, drawing out her name. "Maple," I patted my leg.

Thud.

I winced. *Ok, that sounded close.* "Maple!" My hoarse whisper was tempered with anxiety. I rounded a corner and peered down the stairs. I looked at the front door with longing. So close to freedom. *But I'll go through my window. Safer.*

At the bottom of the stairs, Maple lay curled up on the doormat. "Maple! Come here!" She stared at me, then, after what seemed like an eternity, slowly walked up the stairs to me. "Yes! Yes! Come here!" I patted her as she panted and smacked her lips. "Let's go." I turned and walked cautiously back to my room, checking behind me constantly. Every time she stopped to sniff, I patted my leg with furious urgency. My heart pounded, and my blood painfully rushed into my ears. *Almost there.* I looked into my room and stopped in my tracks. My window was open.

I didn't leave it open. My heart skipped a beat.

Thud. Thud. Thud.

That noise was in my room.

I wheeled around and gathered up Maple in my arms. She wasn't that big of a dog, but her weight made me wheeze. *Remind me to go easy on your treats, Maple.* I charged down the hall and the stairs as fast I could manage, but it felt like I was moving in slow motion. I fumbled for the latch. My sweaty hands had greased it, and it wouldn't turn. *Now. Open NOW.* My breathing was frantic, my blood roaring in my ears, the hair on the back of my neck standing up. It finally clicked, and I flung the door open.

Thud. Thud.

Not daring to turn around, I broke into a run. I squinted against the lashing rain, trying not to slip in the wet, muddy grass. I set down Maple, and she ran beside me as I charged down the front lawn and onto the road. "Come on, Maple!" She barked in response and ran ahead of me as we bolted down the worn and narrow asphalt road. I could hear sirens in the distance, but I did not heed them. I could have sworn I heard footsteps behind me, and I put on a burst of speed. My legs burned and my lungs screamed. I wasn't going to be trying out for cross-country anytime soon.

I could see the porch light of the Harrisons' house now as the sirens grew louder. Maple was barking loudly. I could see lights clicking on within the house. I slowed down a bit, unable to run anymore. Gasping, I took the steps up to their door. I rang the bell repeatedly until the door was opened by one very exasperated Mr. Harrison.

"Allison? What are you doing up? It's 2:30, for God's sake!" But then his face changed. He saw my face. He heard the sirens. "What's wrong? Are you hurt?"

I attempted to speak but could only gasp out words. "Noise...in house...let me...in... *please*," I wheezed, grabbing my chest.

"Sure, sure....Come in." He looked concerned. Not concerned, frightened. More lights clicked on as the sirens got louder. I sat on the floor, head in my hands, shaking. Around me, more of the family who had awakened emerged from their rooms, some yelling at each other, everyone confused. Blue and red lights cut through the deluge, flickering across the windows. Across the street, lights turned on, and doors opened. Maple licked my hair, attempting to get me to look up. I smiled weakly, stroking her head. The background noise faded away, and relief settled in. *I made it.*

The following days were some of the weirdest of my life. My parents came home early from their trip, confused and concerned. I didn't sleep much, and when I did, I'm slightly embarrassed to admit that a nightlight was involved. The cops checked the whole house up and down, and their conclusion never sat well with me. And I'm not a superstitious person, mind you, but what they told me sent a chill down my spine. They told me: "There was never anyone in the house."

This gave me great pause, to say the least. I definitely got weird looks from my parents in the following days, sometimes even catching them conversing in hushed tones, which would abruptly stop if they heard my footsteps. I would lie awake in my bed during the night, alert, stiff and unmoving. My head shot up at every tiny sound, my breathing fast and panicked, sweat beading on my forehead. *Was I going crazy?* This I asked myself more than once.

A few days later, my dad came into my room, early in

the morning. *He's never up this early.* I gave him a cautious stare. "Yeah?" I kept my tone even. *This couldn't be good.* I tried to tamp down my worries.

"Allison, I think I may have found what was causing all that bumping," he told me, relief in his eyes. *Maybe this isn't bad news.* My optimism was cautious. "I think it may have been our HVAC system! That thing is so ancient, I wouldn't be surprised if it had some problems." I felt relief wash over me. *I'm not crazy, and this godforsaken house isn't haunted!* "I've called the repair guy to come look at it," he told me. I smiled and thanked him.

Maybe, just maybe, things were going to be okay.

The next day, I emerged from my room to some happy looking parents.

"It looks like it was the HVAC that was bumping, Allison," My mother told me with a calm, relieved expression. She was probably thinking *Thank God my daughter isn't losing it.* I was thinking it, too. "We've ordered a new one," she told me, and my mood improved significantly. *I'm going to be okay.*

Just to be sure, I went downstairs to where the HVAC guy was working.

"Hi," I said. He turned and nodded. *God, no matter the situation, I am always awkward.*

"So, what was wrong with it?" I asked.

He shook his head. "Nothing, really,"

I felt a chill go down my spine. "What do you mean?"

"I mean, it is very old and in dire need of a replacement, but I couldn't find anything wrong with it."

The nervous energy returned and, even though it was hot down in the basement, I shivered. "Nothing that would make it bump?" I asked. But I knew the answer.

"Nothing."

That night I lay in bed, feeling a bit better. I had spent the better part of the day convincing myself that it was just squirrels in the attic, the house settling, mice in the walls, that storm, anything *logical*. And it had worked. *What would it even be?* I asked myself. *Don't be irrational.* I turned off my bedside lamp and plugged my phone into its charger. Pulling up the covers and rolling onto my side, I closed my eyes and began to drift off. The turmoil of worries in my mind had abated, and I felt the anxiety that had clouded my mind melt away. *I'm going to be okay.* For the first time in days, I believed that statement. I smiled to myself. Just as sleep came to me, I heard it. The hairs on the back of my neck stood up. Any relaxation I felt, any notions of calm or relief, had left me. I was left alone in my room, just me, the noise, and its maker.

Thud.

IF ONLY I HAD LISTENED
By Diana Karakunnel

"Mom, come on. Please, everyone is going. Even just for a couple hours?" I was practically on my hands and knees, begging her to let me go out to meet my friends at the mall. She kept going on and on about this "social distancing" thing and this coronavirus. How bad could it be? My dad had sent us articles in our family group chat daily, and my mom told me about all the symptoms, thinking she'd scare me. I had read some of the articles. It sounded like the flu, so I wasn't too scared. Instead of a simple "no," my parents went on what felt like a years-long rant about how I needed to be studying and cleaning my room and doing homework. But, finally, they gave in.

"Fine. Just for a couple of hours," my mom said.

When I got to the mall, there was barely anyone there, and the few people that were there were wearing masks. Some even had gloves on. I couldn't help but chuckle about how dramatic I felt people were being about this whole "corona" thing. When I found my friends, none of them were in any of those crazy-looking get-ups. We grabbed some food, sat down, and talked. As we finished and started walking around the empty mall, it seemed weird. After a while, we split up and went home.

About a week later, I began to feel a little lightheaded. I didn't want to make a scene, so I didn't say anything to anyone. It went on for a few days. My body felt tight. I was listless. My symptoms began to get worse, and one day I suddenly felt like I was on a Ferris wheel going backwards, and everything went dark. Every few minutes I opened my eyes, but my vision was all blurry. I could see a stretcher. It felt like I was being lifted up. "Who is that?" Wait, the sign up above my head near the top of the building read "Suburban Hospital." *What am I doing here? Oh, my gosh. I'm in the hospital? What's going on?* Everything went dark again.

I opened my eyes, feeling like I couldn't move and hearing quiet murmurs throughout the room—words quiet enough to not even make out—bloody murder screaming and crying, faint buzzing coming from the bright lights above me.

Am I even breathing? What's going on? I couldn't find anyone, and I couldn't move. I tried to look around, but I could barely lift my head because of the weight of the tubes and mask that were connected to machines all around me. I slowly turned my head to the right and saw a group of nurses gathered next to me.

"She has it, for sure."

"Here we go again," they murmured.

One nurse said, "What if she has to be taken off the ventilator? There aren't enough for everyone."

I turned my head towards the left ever so slightly and saw my parents, both wearing masks, staring at me from outside a glass that separated us. My mom stared at me, and I stared back at her. Tears were coursing down her cheeks. Then tears began to fill my eyes. I didn't know what was going to happen. It had to be the mall visit. The guilt of wishing I had listened to my parents and had socially distanced with my friends felt like more weight than all this equipment combined. She looked at me and mouthed the words, "I love you," but all I could do was look back at her with my teary eyes. I couldn't even respond to an "I love you" from my mom. Tears continued to flow down the sides of my face, slowly getting to my ears as little soft droplets.

Hours had gone by, maybe even days, since I had blacked out at home. I didn't even know how long it had been. I had no concept of time, people, things, feelings. It seemed like my mind was reeling through one black hole of nothingness. Every time I woke up from a deep sleep, all I thought was, *if only I had listened.*

Nurses moved around me and asked questions.

"Hi, sweetheart. Do you feel any different?"

"How's the breathing?"

"What are you feeling?"

I just wanted to rip off the mask and pull out the tube going down my throat and tell them I wanted to see my family. I wanted to hold my cats. I wanted to go home. They kept asking the questions, even though they knew I couldn't respond, talking to me like I was a two-year-old, which did not help. Like, look, I can hear you. I just can't speak because I'm intubated. Clearly, what I was feeling was frustration. Doctors trolled the room checking equipment and my "vitals." Whatever that meant.

I began to reminisce about everything. The hours of homework, my mom making me do chores, my dad lecturing me about how eight hours of ACT prep a week wasn't enough. I'd take all of that over this any day. My new daily routine consisted of opening my eyes, staring at the ceiling, and getting questioned by random people for what felt like every ten seconds.

Bit by bit, the feelings got worse. Just taking a deep breath made my chest hurt. It felt like a mix between getting sat on by my cats, the flu, and the beginning of spring allergies all at once, but ten times worse. It was a series of pounding headaches, fever, severe body aches and chills, joint pain, and constant exhaustion. When was it going to end? No one could do anything. All I wanted to do was to be well again and home with my family.

If only I had listened.

CONNECTING DOTS

By Margaret Cravens

Sometimes I like to think about people as billions of little dots of light. Every time you meet someone, a little branch shoots out and connects your dot with their dot as if you influence each other's lives. While you're connected by that little string of light, you become brighter because of it. And even when you have forgotten each other, if that little bond breaks, you're still brighter because of it.

Sometimes I think about it that way. Mostly, though, I just like that idea because I get really sentimental. I don't like letting go. I don't like growing up. I don't like it when people leave. So I tell myself that as long as I remember them, there is still that little string of light connecting us through time and space. And even if I forget them, I tell myself that they'll have made me a bit of a better person.

Sometimes I get baffled by the way humans live. I mean, we're all still animals, aren't we? What gives us the right to kill the planet, discuss philosophy, and create art? It's confusing, but I was just born into it. Still, what gives me the right to write about those issues like I am doing now? And, when you start to think about that, you start to think about the meaning of life. Is it just a bunch of random chemical reactions that separate me from my sweatshirt, a bug from a rock, or is it something more?

And while we are already falling down the philosophical rabbit hole (which brings me back to the whole "why do humans live so differently from other animals" thing), do souls really exist? What is a soul? Is it real, or just something we have made up to explain life?

Maybe this is why I read so much. Fantasy and science fiction give me answers to those questions. Not real answers, but whenever I go into whichever world I so choose, the characters or the magic or the history provide a temporary, pretend answer, and I become satisfied for a while. And maybe this is why I write so much. I want to find my own answer and find a way to share it. Or, maybe I just want to sound pretentious. Who knows?

How much of me is me, and how much of me is being dramatic? That is a question you can't answer. Only I can answer it, but I think I'm afraid of what that answer may be. But, then again, maybe I do know who I am. I know I'm a wannabe rebel who talks big but can never put her money where her mouth is. I know I'm terrified of even slight social discomfort, but that my comfort zone is usually relatively big. I know I care a lot about honesty, and I have a strict moral code. I know I hate to cuss and love to sing, despite not having the greatest skill, and I know I love lots of different things and hate having to specialize. I know I hate tamales and love Kraft mac and cheese, and I listen to weird music that my friends all hate. I know that most people think of me as the grade's little sister. I know sometimes I pretend not to care what people think, but really, I wish people thought of me as an equal. Even my little brother treats me like the younger sibling.

I don't know if I'll ever publish this. I don't know if anyone will even accept it. I mean, it's not really a poem or a short story or a novel piece. But I also know that I like to defy categorization and want to be seen as unique, so there you are.

Maybe you'll read this, and my little dot of light will tie itself to your little dot of light.

Or maybe my whole idea of that is skewed. But I don't want to think of it that way. I want to think that everyone matters to each other, forgotten or not. Because there are people I remember that I only spoke to once, like a girl from a playground many years ago, someone so random; but I remember her. There are people who have been in my life that I don't remember, like those in my kindergarten class picture. I guess I want to think about it that way because I don't want the people who matter to me now to mean nothing later.

I warned you, I get really sentimental.

MY NAME

By Lauren Arianna Raskin

My first name is the color of mud,
the kind that squishes between your toes and gathers in
   the creases of your foot.
The word cannot be tamed by the tongue,
the consonants are far too clipped
while the vowels stretch in all directions.
My first name is the first cloud to appear on a bright day,
the kind that masks the sunlight falling on the ground in
   a single gesture.
It is the sound of a crying child after scraping their knee,
each tear rolling down plump cheeks in a glistening
   cascade.
It is the feeling—the awful emotion—of not having
   anyone's arms to collapse into
when life takes another swing at you!
You feel as if someone took a chisel
and chipped a piece of your heart clean off.

My middle name, however, is one filled with peace and
   hope and happiness.
The tongue waltzes with the word, the sound falling off
   like crisp leaves
tumbling off trees in autumn,
dancing with the breeze as they flutter to the ground.
My middle name is the sight of Christmas lights
   twinkling in the distance,

the merry aura flickering on and off at jolly intervals.
It is the sound of babies laughing for the first time,
their mouths open wide as if they are trying to capture
    the vibrations
traveling through the air
and swallow them whole.

I like to think my personality contains aspects of both
    these names—
this luggage I carry everywhere I go.
I like to think they provide balance for me,
something that occurs too rarely in my life.
The opposites round each other out,
the light to the dark,
the sun to the moon,
the yin to the yang.

But the question we should ask ourselves,
do our names really define us?
These souvenirs of love that our parents chose for us
when we were merely wrinkled balls of flesh,
should we allow them to dictate who we are in the
    present
or what we will become in the future?
Have I already allowed my name to choose who I am?
Well, as for that question,
I suppose only time will tell.

A HELPING HAND
By Ela Jalil

The letter requesting my appearance today was a surprise. Apprehensive, I breathed in the frigid air and exhaled small, misty clouds. The bright image from my yellow puffer jacket stood me in stark contrast to the desolate winter sky, the piles of snow turned gray, and the leafless and dead-like trees that lined the street in their dormant stage. Though I appeared a beacon of light amidst the harsh winter, I dreaded this meeting. Reluctantly, I quickened my pace while rubbing my hands together, trying to warm them as I thought about what awaited when I reached my destination.

As I approached the lawyers' office building, I stopped mid-stride and contemplated. Do I want to go through those doors, or do I want to remain free forever, unburdened with what I might learn that could change everything? I instinctively turned and started to run towards a nearby park. I felt free, taking long, leaping steps, determined to enjoy this day as best as I could, as I would the next day and the days that followed, until I no longer could.

The park was deserted. I had it all to myself, knowing that sensible people wouldn't be out in this weather. I frolicked on the snow atop the brown and lifeless grass, making snow angels, before resting on a bench. I sat there gazing at the still pond. There were no ducks to enjoy; they had flown south in recent weeks. The silence was serene, absent the usual noise of children laughing and shouting as they played. The stillness calmed me as I took off walking down a path. I was so wrapped up in the joy of being alone that I didn't see the patch of ice. I slipped and fell. Besides my bruised ego, there was a twinge in my back. *Thank god no one was around to see me,* I mused.

That moment made me feel alone—but in a good way. No one was around to see my flaws or make fun of me. Or so I thought, because when I started to try to turn over to push myself up, I saw a big glove thrust in front of my face, accompanied by a deep voice, "Gee, miss, are you alright? That was an awful hard fall you had there."

Although my cheeks were already pink from the cold, I turned a deeper shade of red and turned around to see who the hand belonged to. There stood a giant-like man with a large mustache taking up half of his face. His eyes twinkled, and the lines around his eyes deepened as he smiled. I wanted to refuse his hand, but couldn't without seeming rude, so I grabbed onto his leather glove. He pulled me up without breaking a sweat. We stood there in silence, he with a bemused expression on his face as I rubbed my back, where there would be a bruise tomorrow.

"What are you doing out here in the cold," he asked, "besides slipping on ice?"

"If you must know," I retorted, "I was attempting to have the perfect day, and until moments ago, it was."

His eyes twinkled in amusement. He looked like he was trying not to laugh. His mustache started to quiver, and his massive shoulders started to shake, and he finally gave in to the impulse. Attempting to seem above this situation, I stood with my arms akimbo, glaring at this gentle giant chuckling at my expense. Deciding that enough was enough, I turned away and walked off. Anywhere was better than here.

"Wait, miss, I meant no offense," he called out. "I was just wondering what a young lady like you was doing out here alone? It's not safe."

I turned around and eyed him fully for the first time. He was wearing a watch cap and a red parka. Objectively, he would be terrifying—a hulk of man with a scruffy beard obscuring most of his face. But he had kind eyes—eyes that reminded me of my father. Maybe it was this comparison or his genuine concern, but I turned back towards him.

"My name is George," he said, lifting his hands towards me.

"Lisa," I replied, letting his hand envelop mine in a firm shake that again reminded me of my father.

We brushed off snow from the nearest bench, sat down, and began to talk.

"I'm here on business, but I have a beautiful wife and daughter at home," he said with a grin. "Since arriving, I have taken long walks every morning around this park to clear my head and get ready for the day."

We talked at length before I glanced at my watch. I winced. We had been talking for over an hour. The meeting with the lawyers was probably long over. I felt a pang of regret for having squandered the opportunity.

George noticed the look on my face and asked, "What's wrong?"

Can I trust him? I thought. I felt sure that I could. "You know how earlier I said the reason I was out here was because I wanted a perfect day?" I said quietly, looking down at the snow. "Well, really I was avoiding something big in my life, and I thought if I ran from it, it would somehow go away. My mom's will was supposed to be read to me today."

"Oh, honey, I'm so sorry," he said.

"Don't be," I sniffled. "She abandoned my dad and me when I was ten. She ran off with someone else. She never wrote to me, called me, or remembered my birthdays. I had to go through all of my formative life experiences without her. Whatever she left for me in her will would be more than she has done for me in the last ten years. Honestly, I don't think I'm ready to forgive her."

George took my hand, looked me in the eyes, and said three words that I'll always remember. "There's still time."

With that statement ringing in my ears, I stood up. I could try and run away from my problems, but they would always be with me—no matter where I went. I squared my shoulders and shook George's hand. Determined not to look back, I set off to face my future.

ACKNOWLEDGMENTS

This fifth volume of *Emerging Voices: Poetry and Prose by Maryland Teens* was created by a large team of teens and adults to showcase some of the work produced by the Maryland Writers' Association (MWA) Teen Writing Clubs.

Members of Teen Writing Clubs around the state meet regularly at local libraries to share their interest in writing and provide one another constructive feedback. This past spring, when the coronavirus shut down local libraries and forced everyone to remain at home, several teen clubs moved their meetings to online or video platforms and continued to work on their craft.

Members who submit material to be considered for inclusion in the annual anthology work particularly hard to workshop their materials within their groups. Adult editors then guide them with questions and suggestions for revisions. We could not have produced this volume without the help of a team of editors—Henry Caballero, Roderick Deacey, Neal P. Gillen, Christina L. Lyons, and Kari Ann Martindale—who generously volunteered their time and professional skills to judge and edit the submissions. We also are very grateful to copy editor Joanne L. Zaslow and proofreader Mark Willen who also volunteered many hours to help edit and polish all the copy.

Thanks also to the MWA, which sponsors the program. The MWA Board under President Eileen McIntire and incoming president, Amy Kaplan, have been especially supportive, providing advice, encouragement, and financial backing for the program and for this book.

Our teen club leaders volunteer their time and expertise generously. We are very grateful for the contributions of Henry N. Caballero, Neal P. Gillen, Shelby Settles Harper, Ginny Hillhouse, Frank S. Joseph, Christina L. Lyons, Kari Ann Martindale, Stacey Mednick, Carolee Noury, Linda F. Wood, and Joanne L. Zaslow.

We also are grateful to the libraries that co-sponsor the Teen Writing Clubs, providing free space, publicity, and hands-on assistance. The clubs rely on the support of Tessa Gunnell at the C. Burr Artz branch and Cindy Mogel of the Walkersville branch of the Frederick County Public Libraries; Levertes Ragland and Flor Benasayag at the Chevy Chase branch, Susan Cohen and Alicia Hanson at the Germantown branch, Jennifer Meddings at the Gaithersburg branch, Carol Reddan at the Olney branch, Michelle Izuka and Danielle Deaver at the Potomac branch, and Thomas Palmer at the Silver Spring branch of the Montgomery County Public Libraries; Monica Pride Powell at the Odenton branch and Michele Noble at the Eastport-Annapolis Neck branch of the Anne Arundel County Public Library.

Finally, the teen clubs and the anthologies would not be possible without the support of the parents and guardians of our teen club members. They encourage our emerging writers and make it possible for the clubs to flourish.

Made in the USA
Middletown, DE
17 September 2020